To R and R:
You are the ones who made all of this possible.

One

I HAVE MY OWN SHOP!

Kate Morrison grinned at the thought as she emptied the last of the buttons into a jar and placed it on the rickety shelf left behind by the previous tenant. The shop needed work, but it would have to wait. Her first day was spent arranging fabrics and sewing accoutrements. Looking around the open room at the front of her shop, Kate's gaze took in the bolts of fabric that lay on teetering shelves and the spools of thread that covered the limited table space. The floors were scuffed from years of traffic. She couldn't help the wash of pride at her new space, and for what she'd achieved since moving to Brexton, New Mexico only a month ago.

After the Civil War ended, the town's reaction to the slow trickle of men arriving for the increasing coal work had shown Kate just how different her reception had been, even compared to those who just passed through. They were welcome, while she was suspect.

Money was scarce after spending most of what she had earned from previous jobs on getting to Brexton. To make ends meet, she had asked the town physician if he needed any help. The fact that she had medical experience had shocked the older man, but he warily brought her on.

She then used what she could to purchase small bits of fabric to make dolls and dresses for the little girls in town; the little boys had gotten monogrammed handkerchiefs. Their mothers soon began to ask her if she had any experience making women's dresses. Kate had balled her hand in the skirt of her dress to keep in the excitement she had felt at the prospect of getting official customers.

"I have my own shop," Kate said, bringing her hands to her face in delight. She didn't think she would ever get used to saying that.

Joy raced through her. But she was interrupted as the doorbell tinkled. She turned to see a large figure entering the shop.

"Evenin', Miss Morrison," the man said.

Kate willed her expression to stay neutral. "Good evening, Mr. Dixon." She looked down, gripping the edge of the table. *I should have left earlier,* she thought grimly. Mr. Lez Dixon was the last person she wanted to see, other than her own mother.

Mr. Dixon took a few steps into the shop, letting the door swing closed behind him. The distinct stench of overripe body odor and chewing tobacco assaulted her senses. Her eyes welled and her stomach lurched. A small slurp and a squelch filled the silence in the shop as Mr. Dixon chewed his tobacco. When he spit into the corner, Kate fought every instinct to gag. His burly frame filled the space between her tables as he slipped his hat from his head. The sheen of oil clung to his thick fingers as he ran them through his dirty, shoulder-length hair before replacing the hat back in its place.

"I see congratulations are in order fer movin' yer hobby inta town," he said, sauntering closer. Out of the corner of her eye, Kate could see his hands running over the few bolts of fabric she had not yet given a home. *I think I can afford to throw out some of that fabric,* she thought.

"Thank you," she said, turning to face him and lifting her chin. "I have been working towards moving my *business* into town since I moved here."

He chuckled, lifting the brim of his hat slightly and taking another step closer to her.

She kept her face even. Barely.

"Guess it's a good thing I rented the house here by them rock formations stead of the one cross town. Yer a lot closer when I need ya to fix somethin' fer me," he said with a smile that made Kate uncomfortable.

She folded her arms. "Maybe so. But unfortunately, I am not accepting customers today. I have a lot of work to do in this shop before I can open for everybody, Mr. Dixon." She hoped her words were enough to make him leave.

"Don't need nothin' big; just somethin' small." He reached into his satchel and pulled out what appeared to be a vest that had clearly had its buttons pulled off. Reaching in again, he pulled out a pile of buttons. Kate sighed at the items he placed on the table before her.

"Figured I could be yer first customer in the shop." He smiled, leaning towards her and placing his hand on the table between them.

Kate's stomach rolled. As much as she wanted to refuse his request, she needed the business, and every little repair would help.

"Like I said," she finally choked out, "I have lots of work to do in the shop, so I will not be able to get to it for a few days."

"Hope it doesn't take too long, Kate," he said. His eyes roved around the room as he moved ever closer to her.

"You may call me Miss Morrison," she said sharply, taking a step back.

The smile never left his lips, but his eyes betrayed his vexation. "Fine. Miss Morrison." He stepped around the table, and she instinctively leaned away as his hand came toward her face. His hand stopped and his eyes narrowed before he pulled his hand back and ran it across his barrel chest. "Now, don't work too hard. Wouldn't want ya to overdo it on yer first day. After all," he licked his lips, "yer purty delicate."

Kate bristled as the bell tinkled again and Kate watched the carnal look on Mr. Dixon's face transform into a friendly smile before he turned around to see who had entered the shop.

"Hello Miss Morrison, Mr. Dixon," Charlotte Conrad said as she walked in, arms laden with four bolts of fabric. "Found these behind the armchair. They must have fallen and been missed when ya brought everythin' over."

Dixon hurried over to her with a smile. "Let me help ya with those, Mrs. Conrad. Miss Morrison sure is lucky to have a friend like you."

Kate narrowed her eyes. *Why does he change when other people come around?* This man was not what he seemed, but she didn't know who she could talk to about the situation. Mr. Dixon, despite being a new arrival like her, was well-liked by people in town. They all saw the charming happy man before her now. Who would believe her?

Charlotte smiled brightly as he took the fabric. "Thank ya kindly, Mr. Dixon. I admit my arms are mighty tired from walkin' over with these. They didn't seem so heavy when I left the boardin' house, but I ain't as young as I used to be, and I forgot how long that walk can feel."

"Mrs. Conrad, I wish I coulda helped sooner," Mr. Dixon said, carrying the bolts of fabric and leaning them next to the others.

Charlotte chuckled. "Next time I need somethin' transported, I'll surely ask ya."

"I'd appreciate it, ma'am." Turning to Kate, he tipped his hat. "Thank ya fer yer help with my buttons. I'll see ya soon." He sent a suggestive nod to Kate. "Ladies," he said before walking out.

"What a nice man," Charlotte said. "So kind and thoughtful; always willin' to help."

Kate reflected on her own experience with Mr. Dixon. *Would Charlotte believe me if I told her what he was like?* No. She offered Charlotte a lackluster nod.

"I am famished," Kate said, hoping to change the subject. Charlotte began to talk about the meal she'd prepared and how she knew at least one of her other tenants would complain about it. Many men passed through the boarding house on their way home from war, but most just smiled at her and thanked her for the food. Charlotte then mentioned that her son Jesse should be on his way home from the war as well, and he was sure to like her cooking.

Kate hurriedly pulled the dusty curtains closed and locked the door. As they walked home, they discussed Kate's plans. She was grateful for Charlotte's insight into running a business in a small town, and their conversation was soon filled with planning and laughter.

"Thank you for helping me, Charlotte. I could not have done this without you." Kate looked down at the ground as they walked together.

"I know you'll do wonderfully, Kate. I have the utmost faith in yer success."

Kate knew she owed so much to Charlotte. She not only encouraged Kate to follow her dreams, but also helped in any way she could. So, with Charlotte's small financial donation and Kate's promise to fix up the space, she had gotten her lease. Though she felt she owed Charlotte more then she could ever repay, Kate had never felt more free.

Two

Kate was drying the last pot lid after dinner at the boarding house when Charlotte rummaged through her shelves, producing a jar. "Would ya care to join me and this jar of cookies on the front porch?"

"Of course! You know they are my weakness," Kate said, laughing.

Charlotte smiled back. "I know it's getting chilly tonight, but with the summer heat coming soon, I just want to soak in as much cool air as I can."

Both women indulged in the delicious treat after they settled on the porch chairs. Their conversation flowed easily, and Kate wished her relationship with her mother was this pleasant.

"Hello, ladies," A familiar voice called. "May I join you?" Kate could see a petite figure skipping into view, her golden hair flouncing with every step in the fading sunlight.

"Beth Wallace!" Charlotte greeted. "I wondered when you'd come to see me this week. Come sit and have a cookie."

"Don't mind if I do," Beth said, her accent thick as ever. She accepted the treat and sat down.

Kate smiled at her friend. She was the first person Kate had met when she'd come to Brexton. Beth's family owned the General Store, and she'd been working when Kate stepped off the stagecoach and into the store to ask about lodging. Beth had been there, ready and willing to help her with all her needs and tell her all the latest gossip in town.

"Oh, Miss Charlotte! I'm burstin' at the seams! I've read Jesse's letter nearly 100 times today. I check the date over and over, and sometimes I think I calculated it incorrectly and he isn't coming 'til next week. Mama kicked me out of the store today because she said I was bouncin' around and distractin' the customers 'more than usual' whatever that means," Beth said, huffing and pouting.

"Slow down and enjoy the evenin'. Have another cookie." Charlotte offered.

Kate watched Beth gobble her cookie. She knew the delicious confection was the only thing keeping her friend from rambling on.

Kate bit her lips, containing the laugh that threatened to erupt. She glanced at Charlotte and found her doing the same, which almost broke Kate's resolve. Beth, however, took no notice and continued her lamenting.

"Although, he did say he could arrive later than he originally thought. Somethin' about how his friend recently sustained a nasty leg wound on their way home that could slow them down." Beth put her hand on Kate's knee and smiled at the memory of her sweetheart. "Jesse is just the kindest man I've ever met," she drawled.

Charlotte nodded. "That's true," she said with a loving smile. Jesse was her youngest, and only living, child. Charlotte didn't show it often, but Kate knew how desperately she missed her boy and was glad he was on his way home to her. Kate wondered if her own mother missed her so strongly. *Maybe she just missed telling me how to live my life.*

Beth gushed about wanting to make sure Jessie had enough time to rest and recuperate after his travels and about wanting to get married soon after his return. Her emotional spiral continued on and on until she was sobbing into Charlotte's arms about her fears of him not wanting to marry her. Getting to her feet, Kate walked over and put her arms around them both.

After a few moments, Beth pulled away and brushed the tears from her cheeks, a smile on her face. "Thank you," she said.

Suddenly Beth gasped and whirled towards Kate. "Land sakes, Kate! I've been such a ninny and I completely forgot to ask! Did ya get the shop from Mr. Dallas today?"

A small smile formed on Kate's lips as she nodded eagerly.

"Yes, I finally have my own space. And I got it for a bargain." She lifted her head, feeling proud.

"Oh," Beth looked from Kate's smiling face to Charlotte's and then smiled. "That's wonderful news! I must tell ya that some of the people in town didn't think ya could do it, but you did and that's marvelous. Things are lookin' up and I don't think anythin' could dampen this day for ya!"

Kate fought to keep her smile bright. Beth's words had stung somewhat; they also brought to mind a specific pungent odor from only a few hours earlier. Mr. Dixon had been full of insinuations since she first met him. Not wanting to burden her friends with the issues, she had dealt with him herself. So far, diverting him had worked, so that is what she would continue to do. She would take care of herself; that was, after all, what she had always done.

Beth, unaware of the on-going inner turmoil, threw her arms around Kate's neck and hugged her tightly. "I confess, I was hoping you'd get the shop, and then you'd have to stay here fer years and years to come. I desperately hope we can be dear friends forever."

Kate was touched by her sentiment and returned her friend's embrace. "I sincerely agree with you." She was pleased to find that she meant every word.

"And we should find you a beau soon. One who lives in Brexton, so you'll definitely have to stay." Beth said, nodding emphatically.

Kate only offered a stiff smile. She did not want that. Not after Henry.

"You should write your folks back in California and tell them the news." Charlotte said, smiling at Kate.

"Oh, yes! They'll be so proud to hear about your progress," Beth said, clapping her dainty hands in delight, her bright curls bouncing.

Kate nodded, forcing yet another smile. Her heart filled with guilt as she wrestled with her decision to lie to her friends about her life before Brexton. She wanted to tell them the truth, but things were just starting to go right. Would telling them the truth jeopardize the progress she had made?

Keep your secret, her mind whispered. *If you are found, your mother will not let you live this life. You must stay the course.*

Forcing her attention back to the ladies in front of her, she wondered if they would act the same towards her if they discovered she was lying to them.

It's not worth the risk, her mind spoke to her in the dark.

I hope you're wrong, her heart whispered back.

Three

Two days later, Kate smiled as she pulled the door to her shop closed. Her business was slowly building as the women in town showed more and more interest everyday. She turned to link her arm through Beth's, who had been waiting for her to finish for the day. "So, Beth. How has your day been?"

"Oh, Kate. I don't know how I'm ever gonna make it through the next few days. Jesse said he'd be arriving' sometime either tomorrow or the day after, but I find myself starin' out the window any chance I get. Mother's gettin' tired of it. How was the shop today?"

Kate chuckled. Nobody could jump from one topic to the next like Beth. "Things are going well." Getting the shop had been hard and it still needed work, but she was open for business. "In the last two days, I have gotten five dress orders and a number of fabric purchases." She opened her arms wide and smiled. "My business is finally growing."

"That's wonderful," Beth said before giving Kate a knowing smile. "But just wait till you fall in love. I thought I was happy too till Jesse started courtin' me. And there are so many handsome men in Brexton. I'm sure any one of them would do for you."

The smile on Kate's face froze in place as the idea of marriage ran coldly through her. She took a breath. "While I am delighted for your good fortune, Beth, I did not come here to get married. I don't know if I will ever want to."

Beth dismissed Kate's words with a wave. "You say that now, but you'll change your tune when the right man comes along. Mr. Dixon sure seems taken with you. And Jesse mentioned his friend drew the eye of many ladies wherever the war sent them. He must be very handsome.

"Or particularly gruesome," Kate said. The friends giggled and continued walking.

Kate was grateful for Beth wanting her to be happy, but Kate was uninterested in any matchmaking efforts. It wasn't that Kate didn't want to experience love, but she wanted her life to be defined by something more than being a female who had to get married in order to matter.

Boone Carson had been hurting for some time, but he wouldn't admit it.

The gash in his leg wasn't healing like it should and he blamed his horse for constantly jostling it, although he figured a bumpy carriage ride wouldn't have been much better.

"You don't look so good, Boone," Jesse Conrad said. Boone's friend and riding partner had become more insistent that Boone stay in Jesse's hometown for a few days to rest.

"You worry too much," Boone said, forcing a smile. "If it makes you feel better, I'll stay the night and leave first thing in the morning."

"That Reb sliced your leg real bad," Jesse said, his eyes filled with concern. "And he probably never washed that knife a day in his life."

The pounding in Boone's head seemed to increase, but he brushed it aside. "If anything is going to find me laid up for a few days, it's your doctoring skills." Boone's attempt at humor was ignored by his friend. But if Boone was honest with himself, he had grown more worried about his condition as the days wore on.

"We should be at Brexton by this evenin'," Jesse said, wiping the sweat off his brow as he looked at the sun.

"A day sooner than you thought. Could you be impatient to see a certain young lady?" Boone teased, lightly smacking Jesse's arm with the back of his hand. He held in a groan when the movement caused him pain. If Jesse noticed, he didn't say anything.

"You know I am," Jesse said.

"How long is it going to take you to ask her to marry you?"

"Today I reckon," Jesse said with a broad smile on his face.

Boone looked at Jesse. *How is he so excited about getting married?* Sometimes life and love are confusing. "Good. That young lady deserves a medal after having to wait on you all this time." Boone laughed. His thigh throbbed with the exertion and he coughed.

Jesse gave him a sidelong glance but stayed silent.

"You gonna talk to her daddy before you ask her?" Boone asked, trying to fill the silence.

"I asked him before I left."

"And you're sure she didn't find someone else?" Boone turned to face his friend, but pain shot up his leg.

"I got her last letter in Louisiana, just before we left, and it didn't mention meetin' someone else. But if she did in the month we've been travelin', I would keep on riding and go north with you to your family's ranch. I'd work myself to death with you as my taskmaster." Jesse laughed. "But I'll have you know, if you weren't injured, I'd be there already. Shoot, I could've been married for a week by now," Jesse teased, but Boone could see the worry behind his dark brown eyes. Jesse continued. "Beth is the most beautiful woman I ever met. You'll be a lucky man if you can woo someone half as pretty as her."

Boone smiled grimly and shook his head. "You know I ain't planning to woo anyone. I just don't have that drive in me anymore."

"I know what you said. But life has a funny way of handin' you things you didn't think you'd need." Jesse smiled and started whistling an old battle song. They rode in silence for a while with Jesse's whistling and the plodding of horse's hooves the only other sounds.

Boone thought about their conversation and the letter he'd sent to his mama months before. He wondered how she had reacted to his request. So as not to alarm her, he had agonized over every word.

...Mama, I look at my current circumstances and outlook on life, and I know I cannot offer much. I do not know how much love I have to give, but I think you could help me try to at least lead a comfortable life.

This war has taken away any inclination to properly woo and wed a lovely lady. I ask that you take on the task of finding a suitable companion for me upon my return. I am trusting your judgement.

I must say that after writing this request down, I feel relieved. It's as if a burden has been lifted from my chest...

Despite feeling relieved, Boone didn't know if he'd made the right choice. What he did know was that the war had scarred his soul. He wondered if his sweet mama had done as he asked, or if she was waiting to chastise him when he returned

If he returned.

The pain in his head and his leg had worsened in the last few hours, and he was having trouble sitting straight. His eyes drifted to the gash in his leg. It was rimmed with dried blood and oozing white and yellow puss. The skin around the wound was an angry red. He didn't even want to think about touching it. Maybe staying with Jesse for a few days to get the wound looked at would be for the best.

Though the sun was beginning to set, Boone could feel sweat pouring down his back. His water was running low, and his vision was beginning to blur. He hoped they would arrive soon.

Jesse let out a triumphant whoop when they finally saw the distant shape of buildings.

"Go on," Boone said softly, using every ounce of energy on sounding normal.

With a smile, Jesse spurred his horse forward and was gone in a splash of dust.

Boone took the ride slow. With every second, he felt weaker and weaker until he realized he wasn't directing his horse at all. The disappearing heat was making him cold, and his mind clouded with exhaustion.

The pounding of horses' hooves interrupted Kate's thoughts. As the women looked behind them to the edge of town, Beth gasped in excitement and let go of Kate's arm. Squealing, she ran toward the rider, one hand holding her skirt and the other waving frantically in the air.

"Jesse!" Beth's voice was joyful. Kate watched a tall, strong rider come up to Beth and leap off his horse. His dirty blonde hair poked out under his Union hat. He gathered Beth in his arms, holding her close. His hat and scraggly beard shaded most of his face, but his slim body was relaxed as he held her. Beth's fears about her beau were obviously unfounded.

Kate watched the happy reunion until a second rider caught her eye. His horse was moving slowly, and the rider's body was slumped forward over the horse's neck, barely remaining in the saddle. Kate recalled that Jesse's letters mentioned his friend had been injured.

She rushed towards the rider till she was in front of him, and the horse slowed to a stop.

Remembering the medical lessons she'd learned at her father's side, she could see now that his face was too pale and weary. His dark hair and beard were long and unkempt, and he looked underfed, but Kate couldn't deny he was a handsome man.

She shook her head to refocus her thoughts.

Kate worried about the soldier's condition. His uniform coat was unbuttoned, and she could see the shirt below was almost completely soaked with perspiration. He didn't look at her. In fact, his eyes were half-closed.

She took the horse's bridle in her hand, intent on leading it to the boarding house. "You don't look well, sir. You need to lie down."

Time slowed as Boone's remaining energy drained from him. But when his horse stopped abruptly, he heard the melodic sound of a woman's voice. He managed to lift his drooping head and look up.

Boone saw a woman—a very pretty woman. The fading golden rays of sunlight reflected in her dark chestnut hair and her deep brown eyes looked heavenly and warm. He could use something warm right now.

"Mmm," he grunted. *I must be dead if there are angels around.*

The woman moved to lead his horse, but Boone's strength was spent. His body slipped from the horses back and he hit the ground as darkness finally took him.

Four

Kate knelt by the man's side and rolled him over to allow air into his lungs, and to get a better view of any injuries. The rust-coloured stain on his left pant leg gave away the issue.

"Where is Doc? Someone get Doc Jones." Jesse's eyes searched the growing crowd.

"He left last week for Houston," Beth said as her eyes brimmed with tears.

Kate spoke up. "I know how to help, but we need to get him to the boarding house." She hoped the wound wasn't too infected. This man had too much life left to live.

"What can I do?" Beth's face was tear-streaked and flushed.

"Run ahead and tell Charlotte we are coming. Then grab my sewing bag from my room." Kate knew that Beth needed something to do. This would be a lot for anyone to witness, but with Beth's tender nerves, Kate didn't think this was a good thing for her to see.

Several of the men who had been standing around watching now joined in to help Jesse haul the unconscious man to the boarding house. When they arrived there, Kate directed them to the kitchen where she would have space and most of the tools she needed. Once her patient was laid on the table, Kate felt his forehead. He was burning up and she knew that she didn't have a whole lot of time to get the fever and the now apparent infection under control.

"When did this happen?" She asked Jesse as she grabbed some kitchen scissors and cut away at the man's pants. A few of the other men who helped shook their heads or narrowed their eyes at her as they all left.

Jesse looked down at his hands "We were attacked one night on the road home. We thought they were robbers, but we didn't have anythin' worth takin' other than our horses—and they looked just as tired and worn as Boone and I. Boone stopped them, but he was stabbed. I took care of it as best I could." Jesse pointed to the stained bandage that had slipped to just below the oozing wound. "I just didn't think it was this bad."

"Did he ever say anything about it?"

Jesse shook his head. The wound was deep and grotesque. White puss seeped from the edges and inflammation pulled from all sides of the split wound.

"I need you to get a fire going, boil some water, and fetch some soap. If you have it, strong whiskey will help cleanse it as well." Kate said. Jesse moved quickly toward the cellar.

"I already got the fire goin' and here's the soap." Charlotte appeared in the doorway that led to the rest of the house. In her arms she held the soap, a washing bowl, and towels. She placed them on the counter as she walked over to her son and gave him a tight hug. She pulled away quickly. "We'll have plenty of time to catch up after we help your friend." She smiled before Jesse rushed down the stairs to the cellar.

"Do we need anythin' else for this?" Charlotte turned to face Kate.

"I sent Beth to fetch my sewing bag upstairs. But she should be back by now." Kate looked at Charlotte, "Would you mind checking on her?"

Charlotte nodded and moved toward the door she had come from as Jesse came out of the cellar.

"Do you know what you're doing, Kate?" Jessie set the whiskey on another table.

"Yes. I have patched my brother's many wounds since I was young," she said. A pang of grief rushed through her at the memory of her fallen brother.

"And she worked a bit with Doc Jones trying to save up for her own shop," Charlotte said, nodding as she left. Kate smiled and turned her focus back to the man on the table.

She took a hold of the man's hand and squeezed it. "I am sorry for what I have to do. It isn't going to be pretty, but it has to be done or you will likely lose your leg."

Kate was startled when he opened his eyes and jerked her closer. "Tell me your name." The burn of his fever was evident in the warmth of his hands. His grip was too strong for her to pull away and he drew her in.

"Won't ya give me your name?"

Jesse placed his hand on the wounded soldier's arm. "Boone, let the lady go."

"Miss Kate Morrison," she said, breaking free of his grasp.

"Kit?" His eyes glossed over.

"No, it's *Kate* Morrison, and you need to hold still." She pushed him back down.

"When Charlotte gets back, we will need to move quick. The faster we move, the greater chance we have of saving his leg. And his life," she said, filling the bowl Charlotte brought with water. It had been over a month since she'd worked on a serious wound and even longer since she'd worked on one this infected.

She turned back to the table where Boone was now trying to sit up.

"Jesse, I think you are going to have to hold him still," Kate said as she walked to the cupboard to fetch candles. Charlotte entered with Kate's sewing bag and reported that she had sent an emotional Beth to collect clean linens for bandages.

Kate turned back to the room and immediately rushed to the table where Boone was thrashing violently. Jesse was struggling to keep his friend down. Jesse had moved to the side of the table and had thrown his entire body over Boone's midsection in an attempt to immobilize him. Charlotte rushed forward to grab hold of his feet and held on desperately, yet both her and Jesse's attempts were still being thwarted.

Boone was muttering under his breath over and over, "I'm fine. I got this far. I can make it all the way."

"You really need to hold still, I know you are in pain, but we can help you." Kate's voice was gentle.

After a few more futile moments of trying to calm and restrain him, Kate's impatience won out and her bedside manner evaporated. "Oh, for the love of all...This is ridiculous," she muttered. Walking away from the writhing man, she grabbed a large needle from her sewing kit and dipped it in the boiling water. Pulling it out, she turned back, grabbed ahold of his leg, and jabbed it into the side of his thigh.

A bellow of pain flew from Boone's lips and a string of protests spewed from Kate's helpers, but she ignored them all. Instead, she leaned over her now still patient and looked him in the eye.

"Did you like that?" she snapped. His eyes narrowed. "Did you?" she said again.

His eyes bored into her. *The prick of the needle must have cleared his mind for a moment.*

"Good. Now if you don't want to lose either your life or your leg, I need you to hold still, or I will stab you again." She held his gaze for a moment.

In the depths of his eyes, she could see fathoms of darkness and grief she could only imagine. What had the war done to this poor man? She couldn't do anything about that now, but she could try to help his physical injuries. Taking a deep breath, she focused on the task at hand.

"What's your name, soldier?" She forced her voice to soften, trying to distract him from what was about to happen.

"Boone. Boone Carson," he said, closing his eyes and grimacing.

"Listen to me, Mr. Carson," Kate nodded at both Charlotte and Jesse, and they moved back into position, "I know this is going to hurt, but it has to be done, so you may want to bite down on this." She offered him the handle of a wooden spoon and then grabbed the washcloth and soap.

Kate steeled her nerves for what was going to come next. Taking the bowl of hot water she had filled earlier, she walked back to the patient. She focused on the wound, trying to figure out the best way to address it.

Beth appeared with arms full of clean rags ripped into strips and offered them to Charlotte.

"I can't take those right now, Beth." Charlotte said, gripping Boone's feet. Beth dumped the rags into the boiling pot.

"I'm sorry." Kate's voice was barely above a whisper as she poured whiskey over the raw flesh. She heard Boone grunt in pain, his entire body stiffening for a moment before it relaxed again.

Being as gentle as she could, Kate smoothed away the dried blood and grime from around the lesion. A sharp hiss of air came from Boone when Kate got closer to the red and infected area. Moving with as much care as she could, she cleared away everything she could see. Once again, she used the whiskey to rinse the area.

Kate lathered up the soap on the cloth and her hands. Her stomach clenched. Shaking her head, she focused back on the leg. Kate was hesitant to put her fingers inside the infected area, but the man on the table was injured badly and needed her help.

"Here we go." Kate looked at Charlotte and Jesse. They braced themselves against Boone as she moved her hand toward the oozing flesh. The moment the sudsy cloth touched the inflamed skin, Boone stiffened. She scrubbed the edges and surrounding area. Taking a deep breath, she plunged her finger and the cloth into the wound.

Boone's white-knuckled grip on the edge of the table and the gnawing of the wooden spoon between his teeth pinched at Kate's heart.

Kate shook her head as she moved her hand farther into the rotting flesh. Again and again, she lathered, scrubbed, and rinsed with her cloth. Moving around the wound, she tried to get it as clean as she could. It was larger than she had first thought, and after some scrubbing the opening appeared to be almost smooth. The bottom flared wider, giving way to a puss pocket. She could feel the hard smooth surface of bone underneath.

Her stomach rolled violently as the thin membrane surrounding the puss erupted onto her hand. Panic filled her body. Introducing more infection to the area was the opposite of her aim. She had to move quickly. Again, she lathered, scrubbed, and rinsed her cloth and her hands.

"Hold tight everyone. This is going to burn." She nodded toward Jesse; he gripped the edge of the table, squishing the man beneath him even more. Kate poured more alcohol on a fresh cloth and scrubbed one last time.

"I'm almost done, Mr. Carson. I just have to sew you back together. Then you can get some rest." She threaded the needle and dipped both the needle and thread in the whiskey—then the boiling water for good measure—and set to work.

Boone's whole body stiffened and he groaned in agony. Jesse and Charlotte hunkered down and held tighter, grunting with the effort. Beth moved to help Charlotte.

Three stitches down.

The makeshift medical team fell into an uneasy rhythm. Each time the needle pierced Boone's skin, they all tensed. And as Kate pulled the string taut, they all relaxed slightly.

Eight stitches down.

The pained groans fell from the air and the wooden spoon clattered on the table. Kate looked up at Boone in alarm, but relaxed when she saw the steady rise and fall of his chest.

"I think he just lost consciousness," Kate said.

Beth was quietly sobbing now and Jesse was wearing thin. No doubt the strain of the journey home had worn him down and the task at hand sapped the rest of his little remaining strength. Charlotte whispered soothing words to Boone, but everyone took whatever comfort they could from them as well.

Eleven stitches down. Only one more.

Kate felt the perspiration on her forehead and took a moment to wipe it away with her sleeve. She pushed the needle through one last time, but Boone barely flinched. She tied it off and cut the thread. The others relaxed their grips on Boone's body but stayed close. Kate worked quickly to apply bandages, then scrubbed her hands in the bucket of clean water.

"It's done," she said, sighing with relief. Boone's eyes fluttered open for a moment, a tear trail flowing down his temple. A lump formed in Kate's throat. This soldier had already been through so much, and now she had added to his pain. She walked up to him and forced a smile before whispering, "It's done, Mr. Carson." He made no sound and closed his eyes again.

"I know we haven't met officially, but I wanted to thank you, Miss Morrison," Jesse said, getting Kate's attention. He extended his hand, which Kate took as she smiled. "Boone is a stubborn son-of-a-gun for not tellin' me how bad his leg was. We've become fast friends and I owe him my life. I thank you for savin' him."

"It was no problem." Kate turned away, trying to hide the warmth she felt rising to her cheeks.

"You did well," Charlotte said, putting her arm around Kate's shoulders.

"Thank you. We will still have to watch for infection, but he'll survive today." Kate rubbed an ache in her neck.

"I sent Beth to collect a couple extra pillows for Mr. Carson's room. I got the rest of the room settled, but I figured he'd like some extra support for his leg."

"I agree," said Kate.

Beth came into the kitchen, eyeing Boone as he lay sprawled on the table.

"Are the pillows ready?" Charlotte asked.

Beth jumped. "Yes. I piled them at the end of the bed like you asked."

"Thank ya, honey," Charlotte said. "It's gettin' late. Jesse, please escort Beth home," her eyes narrowed, "and come home promptly."

Jesse sent his mother a mischievous smile and crossed the room to Beth and they left.

"Mr. Dawson and Mr. Taylor said they were willin' to help move Boone to his room when you were finished workin' on him. I'll go fetch them." Charlotte said, wiping her hands on her apron.

Kate watched her leave and looked around at the bloody items around that needed to be cleaned. Finally alone, she let out an exhausted sigh and set to work.

Five

Kate and Charlotte had cleaned the medical mess and now stood outside the room Boone had been moved to. It was dark except for the oil lamp near his bed casting a pale light on his sleeping form. Kate thought he almost looked peaceful.

Charlotte spoke first. "Even though he looks better, I'm still concerned about Mr. Carson's condition, so I'll stay with him tonight. You should get some rest. You look done in."

Kate shook her head emphatically. "No. I'll look after him. You have other patrons to care for and your *son* just got home."

"Ya can't do that," Charlotte said, putting her hands on her hips.

"Why not?"

"It's highly improper. I can't allow ya to stay in the same room with a strange man unchaperoned."

"Charlotte, I—"

"And you've a shop to run. Isn't it part of your lease agreement with Mr. Dallas to fix up the shop? How can ya do that if you're dead on your feet?"

Kate sighed. "Charlotte, I can certainly spare one night."

"Can ya? You've financial responsibilities, and ya—"

"Charlotte!" Kate said, holding up her hand. Kate met Charlotte's strong gaze with her own. "You have been so good to me since I arrived, and I need to return at least one of the favors I owe you. Mr. Carson is my patient, and I would like to make sure he lives through the night. And like I said, your son just came home."

Charlotte's intense look softened.

Kate continued. "So, I can care for Mr. Carson while you spend a little time with your son."

Charlotte seemed to consider this for a moment. But she raised her finger at Kate. "It still ain't proper. And if I allow it? What'll people think?"

Kate sighed. "Mr. Carson needs constant supervision right now. I hardly think one night will matter to people. Doc Jones isn't here, and this man would have died if I hadn't intervened."

Charlotte seemed to mull over Kate's logic, but her brow remained furrowed.

Kate sighed. "What if I leave the door wide open and keep a large needle close by?"

Charlotte let out a chuckle. "I admit, I'd feel better if ya did that. And you must fetch me if anythin' goes amiss."

"I will." Kate put her hand on Charlotte's arm. "Don't worry, I will be fine. I think in his weak and fevered state, he won't be able to get out of that bed by himself. And do you really think your son would keep a scoundrel as a friend?"

Charlotte's mouth turned up into a small smile. "I should hope not."

Kate took her friend by the shoulders and softened her voice. "Don't you dare feel guilty about sharing the responsibility. You should try to enjoy the rest of the evening with your son."

Charlotte nodded. "I'll check on ya before I turn in for the night."

Kate nodded and the women exchanged a warm smile. Even with all the bother, Kate secretly enjoyed being lovingly mothered. She could not remember the last time she'd felt that way.

Once Charlotte had left, Kate propped the door open with a footstool then walked over to dim the oil lamp. But her curiosity about this Mr. Carson overpowered her and, using the warm light of the lamp, she took the opportunity to simply look at the man whose misfortune had caused such a commotion.

His knotted hair was coated with dust and perspiration. His lips were chapped and open slightly, his breathing deep and regular. She focused on his nose, which she noticed had been broken before. Kate wondered how it had happened. Her gaze trailed down his tattered and dirty Union uniform. There were quite a few dark stains amidst the blue that Kate surmised could only be blood. She shivered and tried not to think about how they got there.

Looking at him now, Kate was sure she would be safe from him. He was weak from the wound and from her vigorous intervention. Those, combined with the fever he was now fighting, meant that the threat he posed to her would be as vicious as a toddler learning to walk. He wouldn't have the strength to stand, let alone hurt her.

Still, he intrigued her, and she watched him while he lay sleeping. In one moment, his expression would be still and peaceful and the next, his face would contort into a grimace. Kate felt sorry for the man, despite his fighting her help earlier.

She leaned closer and listened to his breath rise and fall. "I don't think you are a scoundrel, Mr. Carson, but you sure look like one," she whispered.

Suddenly he moaned, and his eyes squeezed tight. He began moving around and twisting the covers.

Kate put a hand to his forehead and noticed it was soaked with sweat. "You need to fight this, Mr. Carson," she said. She crossed the room to dip a cloth in the cool water of the wash basin on the table. As she walked back to his side, she said, "I did not do all that work on your leg so you could die from a fever."

Gently she placed the cloth on his forehead and moved it around.

Without warning, his eyes flashed open and seemed to stare at her, a pained expression behind them. He stilled for a moment and Kate offered a feeble smile in support. He groaned and his eyes closed once more.

Boone's mind jumped from one thing to another. Visions of his peaceful life before he left to fight mingled with the horrible memories of the death and mayhem he endured in the war. Mangled and twisted bodies dissolved into a desert and an attack. Every time he wanted to move his leg, he felt that knife over and over again. He tried to fight the attackers, but it was like his legs were loosely bound.

Every bad moment since he'd enlisted in the Union army played constantly in his mind. One event would latch on his mind and he'd silently beg for mercy until it changed to something worse. Whispers of water and needles weaved themselves through his haunted visions. He tried to call for help, but his voice would only offer nonsensical groans and mumblings.

Through the bedlam in his mind, he would see glimpses of the angel who had spoken to him before he fell off his horse. Sometimes her face was kind, sometimes worried, sometimes fierce. He thought her name was Kit and he thought it was a strange name for an angel. Faded memories of this angry angel stabbing him swirled in his mind. Maybe she was the angel of death. Boone wondered if he should be fighting or following the urge to go with her to whichever end was waiting for him. Every glimpse of her brought a coolness to his mind, but no matter how much he wanted it to, the coolness never stayed long.

Time seemed lost to Boone, but he kept wandering through his mind, searching for a moment of peace. Gradually, he managed to find one, then another and another until the angel and the nightmares faded away. The only thing that remained was the question of a scoundrel. *Had someone called him that?*

Kate smoothed the locks of hair that had fallen out of her bun before noticing the oil was nearly gone in the lamp. Sighing, she leaned back in the armchair and pulled a quilt over her legs.

It had only been a few minutes since his fever broke and Kate felt the exhaustion put its full weight on her. He'd tossed and muttered incoherently all night. Kate had constantly been running to gather more cool water to bathe his face and neck. Occasionally he would open his eyes and look around in confusion.

Kate saw his blankets were low on his body again. Leaning forward, she pulled the sheets back to his chin, making sure he was warm enough. She relaxed back into the armchair. Her eyelids began to close and she welcomed the rest. If she dozed off, Kate was confident any noise he made would wake her. Before she knew it, her eyes shut and she fell asleep.

Boone's mind became alert to a presence next to him. When he tried to look over, his head hurt too badly and he stopped immediately. His body felt battered and bruised, and his head pounded while his mouth and throat felt like a desert. The sky was still dark, but the promise of a sunrise was evident.

He tried to piece his memory together but found it unreliable. Looking around, he discovered he was in a clean and cozy bedroom with lace curtains on the windows, a bureau against the wall, and a wash basin on the desk in the corner. He remembered the presence he'd felt earlier and turned his head, but the effort proved to be painful again. Boone's curiosity overcame his pain and he managed to turn his head.

He was shocked to find that the angel from his chaotic dreams was curled up in the chair next to him, fast asleep.

Obviously not a real angel. She had dark circles under her eyes and her hair was disheveled. Her head rested in her hand and her feet were tucked under her legs. The blanket wrapped around her was slipping and half of it lay on the floor.

Boone just watched her sleep and gradually the fragmented pieces of his day started to become a little clearer.

He'd fallen and been taken someplace where this woman operated on his leg, and he was filled with admiration. But a sharp memory of her stabbing him came to the forefront of his mind and he grew more annoyed.

"You stabbed me." He meant to say it forcefully, but his voice was too dry, and it came out as a croak.

Surprisingly, it was enough to wake her. The not-real-angel's eyes snapped open and she leapt to her feet, coming over to him. Her hands touched his forehead and cheeks. He watched her worried expression soften, followed by what he assumed was a sigh of relief.

"Your fever didn't come back. I was really worried for a while last night, but you are a tough soldier." She gave him a smile.

For a moment, Boone took in how pretty she was, especially when she smiled, but he grew more irritated as more fuzzy memories began to shift into order. She had pushed him, stabbed him, and yelled at him and the knowledge fueled his aggravation.

"I need water," he said, his voice still hoarse.

"Oh, of course." She hurried to the other side of the room and poured a glass from the pitcher. She brought it to him and moved to help him sip.

Boone refused her help. "I'm injured, not a child."

The woman frowned at his raspy words but held the water out for him to take. Boone snatched the glass from her and finished it in four long gulps.

"I am glad to see you are feeling better this morning, Mr. Carson," she said, putting the glass on the desk and sitting in the chair. "We were worried you would not make it through the night."

Boone said nothing. He scrutinized her for a while. He noticed she started to squirm, and a pretty blush tinted her cheeks. The sight of it warmed him somehow, which further annoyed him.

"You're Kit...right?" he asked.

She seemed to bristle at that. "Actually, my name is Kate. But you may call me Miss Ki—Miss Morrison." She stared down at him but seemed flustered.

"Sure. So, you're the one who put me through so much pain last night?" He glared at her, sending all his anger in her direction.

Her mouth dropped open and the red on her face deepened. "I beg your pardon?"

"You're obviously no doctor. I remember you stabbed me with a needle and yelled at me. You either have the world's worst bedside manner, or you're not a real doctor." Boone tried to shout, but his throat was still sore. His mama's voice came into his mind then. He could hear her admonishing him for speaking that way to a lady. He ignored her. It would be easier to blame the not-angel, not-doctor for his discomfort.

"I cannot believe this. I am sorry if I caused you any additional pain, but I saved your life last night." Her face dropped into a scowl.

"And who put you in charge of people's lives? Why wasn't someone more qualified here?" he asked.

She stood abruptly. "I may not be a doctor, but I know what I'm doing. And Dr. Jones knows that too." She stomped to the door.

"Then why didn't *he* take care of me?" Boone asked.

She whirled around. "Because he's out of town!" She pointed her finger and glared at him. "Next time you almost die of infection, I'll be sure to let you!"

"Have a good day, Miss Kit," he said, folding his arms across his chest and returning her glare.

Her hands clenched into fists. "It's Miss Morrison."

He chuckled and looked at the ceiling. "Whatever you say, Miss Kit."

"Ugh!" He heard her slam his door.

"Maybe you shouldn't stab people with a needle," Boone said to the empty room.

"Infuriating man," Kate muttered as she went to the kitchen. Yes, her methods had been unconventional last night, but they had worked. She slathered a piece of bread with jam and gobbled it down angrily. She had hoped for a little gratitude, not such blatant disdain for her efforts.

She stood in the kitchen for a few minutes trying to calm herself. Glancing over at the shelves, she groaned when she realized she'd have to bring him breakfast. She muttered under her breath as she prepared the small meal. Her thankless patient needed to build his strength or all the effort she spent trying to save him would be wasted. She took a deep breath when she approached his room and knocked softly.

"Yes?" came the sharp reply.

"It's Miss Morrison," she said, hoping he had found some manners.

"What do you want?"

Kate took another calming breath. "I brought you something to eat."

He was silent for a moment. "Come in," he said quietly.

Kate sighed in relief before entering the room.

But her smile quickly faded when she saw him standing by the desk and using it to support some of his weight.

"Lie down this instant! You need to stay off your leg as long as possible." She placed the food on the desk and grabbed his arm, attempting to pull him back to his bed.

He only scowled at her and made no effort to move. "I'm out of the army and done following someone else's orders."

"Well, you had better listen to this one. You need to let your leg heal." Kate glared at him and he glared right back. But Kate had no intention of relenting.

He heaved a great sigh. "Say I listened to you. How long would I need to rest?" He spat the last word out like a curse.

"It needs to heal so it won't split open when you walk or sit up. That means a week—maybe two."

His scowl deepened, but he said nothing.

"I know it's not ideal, but this is a terrible injury. You do not want to set your progress back and be required to stay down even longer. Infection could set in again if you move around too soon."

Boone folded his arms in front of his chest and har-rumphed. "My family is expecting me to come home soon. I can't stay here long. And I still don't see why I need to listen to you."

Kate took another calming breath and handed him the cup of water. "If I tell you, will you lie down?" She had no intention of telling him how she'd really gained her medical knowledge, but she needed him to cooperate. As ungrateful as he was, she didn't want him to die.

He nodded reluctantly.

"Good."

After he was in the bed and chewing on his bread and jam, Kate sat in the armchair and began talking quickly.

"I grew up with a rambunctious brother who used to find himself in one scrape after another. He used to drive my mother to insanity whenever she caught him after his escapades, so I learned how to tend to his injuries." It was only a half-truth, but she'd gotten good at pushing the guilt away for telling this same lie to the others in Brexton. "So, when I moved here, I offered my help to Dr. Jones. He and the town now know of my capabilities, and I am quite competent in medical emergencies should the need arise." She sat a little taller when she finished.

Boone ate his food silently, but his scowl had softened. "What's his name?"

"My brother?"

He nodded.

She paused and a lump of emotion swelled in her throat. "Monty. My brother's name was Monty."

"Was?" Boone asked quietly.

"He was lost in the war," she whispered.

They sat in silence for a while and Kate took the time to pull herself together again.

Kate cleared her throat. "Now will you take my medical advice, Mr. Carson?"

After a pause, he nodded once. "But I ain't happy about it. Or that you stabbed me."

Kate sighed in frustration. "I don't relish using such force on you, Mr. Carson. But I did what I had to do to help you and I am not sorry about that." Kate used as much strength and confidence as she could. She was proud of herself for not losing her temper on this man like she wanted to. With that, Kate left the room, but when she closed the door, it slammed harder than she was intending.

No sooner had she done so than she heard him call out, "Temper temper, Miss Kit."

Kate groaned at the door and whirled around, intending to find Charlotte and ask if she would take over.

But a rush of ice filled her body when she saw that Mr. Dixon was waiting in the parlor. He looked up and smiled when Kate entered. She knew it was early, but she wished at least one of the other tenants was lounging in the parlor.

"Morning, Kate," Mr. Dixon said. His smile was lustful, and his eyes roamed unabashedly over her, making her shudder.

Kate didn't move. "It's Miss Morrison."

He huffed. "I stopped by yer shop just now but ya weren't there." He moved toward her. "I need my vest back."

Kate moved, trying to put something between them. "My apologies for the inconvenience. It's back at the shop," she said, trying to keep her face blank.

He nodded at Boone's closed door. "Who's in that room and why were ya yellin' at each other?" A nearly indiscernible sneer crossed Mr. Dixon's face.

"It's just someone in need of medical attention who I offered to help." Kate didn't want to talk to Mr. Dixon any more than absolutely necessary.

"How mysterious. Yer makin' me curious," he prodded.

"I am afraid that I will have to disappoint you." *Now and as often as possible,* she thought.

"Did ya get a chance to fix my buttons?" He advanced toward her again.

"Like I said, it's at the shop." Kate moved behind the couch, trying to maintain as much distance as she could. But it wasn't enough. She could hear the thick wad of chew slosh around his foul mouth.

"Then I'll make sure I come by the shop again." He now stood on the other side of the couch.

Kate could only nod.

"I'll be seein' ya later then, Kate." His smile was far too familiar and it made Kate's skin crawl.

He turned to leave but stopped when he reached the front door. He looked back at her once more and licked his lip. "Yer lookin' perty today. I could eat you up," he said, softly. He laughed and pulled the door closed behind him.

As soon as he was gone, Kate released the breath lodged in her throat as she slumped against the couch. She could feel hot tears threatening and she blinked them away in frustration.

Once she calmed herself, she hurried upstairs to talk to Charlotte as she'd originally planned. "Can I speak with you?" Kate asked after knocking on the door. Charlotte was no doubt almost ready to begin preparing breakfast.

The door opened and Charlotte stood there, twisting her hair into a bun. "Good morning, Kate. What is it?"

"Mr. Carson is not dead, but he is not happy. I am going to sleep until lunch then go work at the shop. I'll stay there through dinner. Could you keep an eye on him?" Kate said in a rush.

"Of course. You look dead on your feet. I'll make sure you're up for lunch."

Kate thanked her and promptly went to her own room. She removed her shoes but didn't bother with changing her clothes. She plopped down on her bed and sleep overcame her as soon as she closed her eyes.

Kate woke to a gentle knocking on her door. She had a dull headache and felt like she'd only slept for a few minutes.

"Kate, it's nearly time for lunch," Charlotte said through the door.

"Thank you, I will be right down." Kate sat up and stretched. Sleeping in the armchair earlier had made her neck and back sore.

She dragged herself from the bed and washed her face. After changing her wrinkled clothes and fixing her hair, she rushed to the dining room and spoke with the other tenants for a few minutes while eating a delicious meal.

She took her dishes to the kitchen and told Charlotte she was going to check on Boone before going to her shop.

She stopped in front of his door to steel her nerves and then knocked softly.

"Come in," came his reply. The baritone of his voice sounded unexpectedly pleasant, but she brushed the thought away and entered his room.

"I am going to my shop now, but I wanted to check up on you. How is your leg feeling?"

"You have a shop? I thought you practiced medicine." He looked at her quizzically.

"I don't have time to talk about that right now. I just wanted to see how your leg is doing."

"I'm fine and don't need your fussing. And where's Jesse? I wanna talk to him about leaving me in such irritating hands." A small smile seemed to contradict his words. Was he joking?

The combination of evading Dixon, having so little sleep, and Boone's words pushed Kate to the brink; she was too tired to fight with him. She rubbed her forehead trying to lessen the pain growing there and sighed. Kate needed her rest, but she couldn't just leave her work for later. She was a new shop owner and that was no way to run a business.

Sighing, she shook her head, avoiding the need to look straight at Boone. "I don't know where Mr. Conrad is, but I will let his mother know you are looking for him. Please stay off your leg. That is the only thing I will nag you on." She tried to keep her voice even, but her exhaustion was evident.

He was quiet for a moment. "Miss Kit?"

"Miss Morrison."

"Right, sorry." His voice seemed different now: softer and kind.

Kate glanced up.

He sighed and met her gaze with his own. "While I'm not thrilled about some of your methods, I am grateful that you saved my life and I'm sorry for how I spoke to you. It was uncalled for." The humility in Boone's voice caught her off guard.

From their brief conversation, she'd branded him hot-headed and irritating, but the man before her was truly contrite. She was further confused by the little jump her heart made when he'd voiced his appreciation.

It took her a moment, but eventually, she found her voice again. "Thank you, Mr. Carson. I am sorry for what I said to you in anger."

He nodded and offered a small grin. She returned it before leaving the room and closing the door quietly.

Kate shook her head as she walked out of the boarding house. She knew she would need to keep a sharp eye on this man. In less than a day, he'd frustrated, angered, intrigued, and confused her.

Six

Kate stretched on her way home from work. Her shoulders and chest still ached from sleeping in her dress earlier, and her fingers were sore from the sewing she had done both the night before and today. Walking up the steps to the boarding house, she slowly let the night air slip between her lips and fill her lungs. Her stomach gurgled slightly as she made her way into the parlor. Charlotte was just calling the other patrons for dinner when she noticed Kate.

"Oh Kate, dinner is ready, if you'd like to join us." Her genuine smile warmed Kate.

"I will. I just want to check on Mr. Carson first."

"I was just in there. He seems to be better, but still a bit tired."

Kate nodded as she headed toward Mr. Carson's room at the bottom of the stairs.

I wonder what his manner will be like now.

The door stood slightly ajar as she neared and poked her head in.

One of the windows was open in the room, letting in the gentle breeze. Boone was sitting up in bed reading a book. "How are you feeling Mr. Carson?" Kate asked as she approached, before stopping. *Was this the same man she had worked on the night before?* His beard was shaved, and it looked like his hair had been washed and combed.

A small smile pulled at the corner of his lips and his eyebrows arched. "Better."

She made her way toward him; her eyes never left his.

"That is good to hear." She said, coming to the edge of his bed.

"May I?" she indicated his leg and he nodded.

With swift and practiced fingers, she untied the bandage. The wound was still red, but no new signs of infection could be seen.

"I should clean it again to keep infection away." Her voice sounded mechanical even to her own ears.

She moved toward the wash basin, picked up a clean white cloth, and began ringing it through her hands, the rivulets of water running between her fingers.

"If you must."

Once she was back at his side, she let her eyes meet his for the briefest of moments before she focused once again on the task of cleaning the wound and rebandaging it.

"Well, it looks good." Kate finished and moved toward the door.

"Wait." The concerned tenor of his voice made her turn back to see him watching her.

"Who was the man from this morning?"

Kate looked at him surprised. "No one. Just a man who needed help with the buttons on his vest."

"Really?" His voice dripped with sarcasm; his lips pressed into a line.

"Yes, it was nothing," she said, waving her hand in the air. Trying to convince herself as well as Mr. Carson.

"Maybe you're right," he said rubbing the back of his neck. "I had been pretty out of it. Then again, I do remember someone calling me a scoundrel," he said. A hint of a smile pulled at the corner of his lips.

Kate could feel the heat of a blush rise. "Well, I don't know anything about that," she said, turning away from him to hide her flaming cheeks.

The low rumble of his mirth made her turn back. "That color suits you, Miss Kit," he said.

"It's Miss Morrison if you please." She pressed her lips together. *Is this how he really is? This was not the same man I worked on last night.*

"Nah, I think Kit suits you," he said with a half-smile once again pulling at the corners of his mouth.

It was Kate's turn to harrumph as she closed the door behind her and walked toward the kitchen in search of something to eat. But before she could get there, Beth burst from the parlor, the echo of disgruntled patrons flowing in her wake.

"Oh Kate, you will never guess what just happened!" Beth said. It didn't take much to excite Beth, but Kate had never seen her friend like this. She was jumping up and down with the biggest grin on her face. The fact that Jesse meandered in only moments later gave Kate a fair guess as to what had happened.

Kate smiled.

"Oh, I can't wait for you to guess," Beth said as she grabbed Kate by the hands and danced in a circle. "He asked me to marry him! Today! This mornin'! Isn't it just the most beautiful day you've ever seen?" Beth sang.

Kate laughed. "That didn't take long at all." Beth bounded around Kate and hugged her.

Then Beth stopped and became profoundly serious. "Kate," she said, taking Kate's face between both of her fluttering hands. "Will you make my wedding dress? Some of Mother's friends asked if I was sure I wanted you to make it, and I couldn't think of anyone better!"

Gratitude filled Kate as she smiled at her friend. "Yes, of course! I would love to." Her mind was already racing with ideas that would suit Beth perfectly.

"What are you thinking? Lace, ruffles, embroidery?" Kate was overwhelmed by her friend's trust with such a special project.

Beth had a small gentle smile on her face as she walked into Jesse's arms. "I've a bit of lace I'd love to use, but other than that..." Beth shrugged.

"I am thrilled for both of you. You will be the most beautifully dressed bride this town has ever seen. When is the wedding?"

"We're thinkin' the end of June," Beth said, gazing at Jesse dreamily. Jesse nodded. "It'll be a bit of a rush to throw everything together in just over a month, but I am sure we can make it work."

Beth's face brightened with adoration and she kissed Jesse's lips briefly. Some of the other patrons in the room behind them watched in barely hidden distain at the display of affection, and Kate cleared her throat, also feeling awkward.

Kate continued their interrupted conversation. "So, do you want a big wedding? Or have you not planned anything yet?"

"I have ideas," Beth said quietly, looking at Jesse.

"Don't look at me, dear. I'll leave the decisions up to you. Except, I do have two requests," Jesse said.

"Anything, my love," Beth said. Kate rolled her eyes and smiled.

"One, I will be the groom at this wedding," he teased.

Beth giggled. "Done!"

"And second, I want us to be photographed. I want the day captured in all its glory, and what better way to have it preserved than with a picture?" He lifted one of her hands to his lips and kissed the back of it gently. The pinch of Kate's heart brought back the memory of the last photograph her mother had insisted be taken of her.

Giddy with excitement, Beth smiled. "Done, my love. Done."

"I'll go tell Boone. You two can talk details." Jesse turned to Boone's door. "Did he give you any trouble?" Jesse asked as he lifted his hand to knock.

Kate shrugged. "Nothing I couldn't handle."

Before Jesse could follow through, Boone's voice bellowed from behind his bedroom door. "Did you say something about a wedding?"

"Ya heard right, Boone," Jesse said, opening the door. Kate and Beth followed Jesse into the room.

"I'm feeling a mite better than this morning," Boone said, lifting himself onto his elbows.

Kate shook her head. "He still needs a lot of time to recuperate."

"Are ya sure?" Jesse asked, turning back, a look of concern on his face. "He sure looks better to me."

"Yes. He's not nearly as bad as this morning, but we need to keep a close eye on his leg to prevent further infection," she said, putting as much authority into her voice as possible.

"I just needed a nap."

"Clearly, you need another," Kate said.

"Maybe later," Boone laughed.

"Boone, I gotta ask," Jesse said. Stepping forward, his hands clasped behind him. "Will you be my best man?"

"Boy, you don't waste any time, do you? Of course, I'll be your best man."

"Wonderful!" Jesse said, clapping his hand on Boone's shoulder. Boone's expression changed suddenly, and he became pensive. "When is the wedding?"

"End of June," Jesse said.

Boone looked at the floor, his eyes narrowed.

"Is that a problem?" Beth stood in the doorway of the room. Her hands pulled at a piece of her dress skirt.

"Well, no, not exactly." Boone looked from one person to another. "My mama just might worry."

"That's easily taken care of. Just write to her that you're stayin' for the weddin' and you'll be home after." Jesse smiled.

"Well, I have other obligations with my family that need to be taken care of as well." Boone wouldn't look at any of them. "Perhaps if I left this afternoon, got my affairs in order at home, and then came back in time for the wedding, I could make that work." Boone was nodding as he tried to pull himself into a sitting position.

Kate stepped forward. "You most certainly will not be leaving this afternoon, Mr. Carson. You have a hole in your leg, and it needs time to heal. You will not be doing anything for at least a week, and even then, you will not be getting on a horse anytime soon." Her voice was stern.

Heat rose to her cheeks as she realized that everyone was staring at her. Straightening her spine and taking a deep breath, she tried to not let the judgments running through her own head change what she knew was best for the patient.

"Fine, I'll stay," Boone said, meeting her gaze. "But only if Miss Kit agrees to help with my recovery."

"It's Miss Morrison." Kate couldn't look away. New light had surfaced in his eyes that made Kate smile, and the smile that lifted his lips in response made her heart flutter. Her chest warmed at the thought of spending more time with him.

Seven

Kate pushed at the ache in her lower back, grateful she was almost finished for the day. It had been a little over a week since Beth and Jesse announced their engagement and Kate had spent every spare minute working on the wedding dress. Beth's tastes in fashion weren't extravagant, but she insisted Kate incorporate her grandmother's lovely handmade lace piece.

Stitching it into the bodice just now had irritated a previously dormant sting in Kate's heart. She had never known her own grandparents because they had lived too far away or had passed on. The last one, her maternal grandmother, passed a year before the war started. Kate's mother, Gertrude, didn't speak of her own mother often, but the few times she had, Kate deduced that their relationship had been strained to the point of not having any association with each other.

Kate had often wondered what Grandma Kathrine was like. She'd always felt a camaraderie with her. Sometimes, Kate would speculate that it was Gertrude's fault for the estrangement, and that made Kate and her grandmother similar, just like their names.

Kate clenched her teeth

She also wondered what her late grandmother would have given her for her own wedding. *Would I have been happily married by now if Gertrude hadn't been so intent on dictating my entire life? She tried to marry me off but instead, she drove me away from it!*

Kate had become so engrossed in her thoughts that she accidentally pricked her finger with her needle. She pinched the spot and waited for the sting to lessen. "I am a seamstress," she said with a dry chuckle. "I should not be poking myself anymore."

She had known that she wanted to be a seamstress since she was 14, but that was not good enough for Gertrude. It was her duty to marry well, not follow dreams, because their family had a reputation to uphold. Her mother had never failed to remind Kate that her goal was the utmost rebellion, and she was a disappointing child because she didn't do everything she was told.

Kate had tried. At least she thought she had. Even though she knew her engagement to Henry was arranged, he still chose to disgrace her when he'd run away with her mother's money. That was the only time Gertrude was more disappointed in someone other than Kate. Not because the betrayal crushed Kate, but because she couldn't control Henry either.

Kate had known she could take no more when she discovered her mother had arranged another marriage. Kate refused to be manipulated like a puppet and left the next week. After all, since her brother Monty had died, she had no reason to stay.

Feeling the anger and hurt building up in her as the memories of her previous life came to her mind, she stood and began vigorously cleaning her workspace.

Kate had long ago determined that her mother didn't love her. Gertrude loved her life, her station, and her influence, but not Kate. Exercising control over others only contributed to that. But it must have infuriated her when Kate ran away. Would it have been so horrible to let Kate choose for herself?

Putting the last of her supplies and tools away, Kate locked up and left her shop. As it faded behind her, the anger and hurt she'd been stewing in began to melt away at the thought of seeing Boone. Their interactions had become something she began looking forward to.

Surprisingly, Boone had listened to all of her recommendations. They had fallen into an easy routine where she would check his wound every morning before work, every afternoon at lunch, and every evening before bed. During those times, they began to talk. The conversations started slowly with small talk and polite questions, but they had gradually shifted to be longer and more interesting. She began to notice how his demeanor toward her, and life, had shifted. He used to be angry and brooding, but now he would fall into fits of laughter, and Kate found herself looking for ways to make him laugh. He was easy to talk to and she felt he truly listened to what she said.

Kate turned the corner onto Brexton's main thoroughfare, and she could see the boarding house at the end of the road. A jolt of excitement went through her knowing another conversation with Boone was near. She quickened her pace.

She had learned Boone's family owned a ranch in Nevada. Having grown up in a large city, Kate didn't pretend to understand the specifics of ranch life, but apparently his father had developed a new technology that revolutionized the ranching industry, which had earned his family some prominence in the area.

He filled her mind with stories about him and his brother and the different scrapes they used to get themselves into. Each time, her heart would hurt for Monty, but then Boone would pull his sleeves or shirt up to show her the scars. Heat would fill her face and she couldn't bring herself to look directly at him. She tried to scold him, but he would only laugh and tease her for blushing.

It was positively scandalous, but Kate secretly enjoyed it. Even though she always left the door open, Kate was sure Charlotte would chastise them if she saw. However, Kate was glad neither Charlotte nor any of the other patrons caught them in those moments because she didn't want Charlotte to stop Kate's visits with Boone. In the privacy of her own mind, Kate allowed herself to think of him by his first name. She wouldn't dare say so out loud. If she did, Charlotte would surely suspect something.

Because of Boone's growing openness and friendliness, Kate wanted to reciprocate, but she kept quiet. There were details about her life that she didn't feel ready to share with people. At least not yet. She didn't want Gertrude to find her, and she didn't know how to tell her new friends why she lied to them. Boone would ask her questions about her life and family, but she managed to evade them. She knew her tactics didn't fool him, but he would smile and allow her to redirect the conversation and it made her grateful.

That wasn't the only thing he did to make her feel more comfortable. He insisted that Jesse bring in the soft armchair from the parlor so Kate would have a nice place to sit as she checked his leg. But they always ended up talking after her evaluation, so eventually Kate just brought her sewing with her and worked while they talked. She had told him all about her shop. Instead of scoffing when she relayed the struggle she faced to acquire and keep the shop, Boone expressed his admiration for her hard work.

Kate was almost to the boarding house. In just a few minutes, she'd be inside talking with Boone again. She looked west, past the building, to the disappearing sun. Only a sliver remained on the horizon and in less than an hour, it would be completely dark.

In some of their more serious talks in the evening, Boone spoke about the war and how it had affected him. He withheld many details for her benefit, but she knew it helped him to talk about the horrors he'd seen. While they were not her favorite things to think about, she was honored that he felt comfortable enough to share his thoughts and fears with her.

Kate's own view of Boone had changed so much in the last week. Even though she still kept many things to herself, she had begun to open up to him. She told him more about Monty and growing up together and they found a bond over the things the war had taken from them.

Lately, he'd begun asking her for her opinion about different topics. They were increasingly random and seemed to come from his mind on a whim. He would challenge her opinions and through their debates, Kate became more secure in her view of life. Gertrude had only questioned her views to prove her wrong, but whenever Boone challenged her, he would validate her opinion. Not only that, but he usually shared them as well.

Getting to talk with Boone had quickly become the best part of her day and now she was home—almost with Boone.

Kate entered the boarding house and hurried to her room for her personal sewing things. Before she left, she glanced in the mirror to fix her hair and check her dress. Shaking her head at her silliness, she left the room and headed down the stairs.

When she arrived at Boone's door, she knocked three times quickly, as she usually did.

"Come in, Miss Kit."

She smiled at his recognizing her knock and she entered the room. She saw him slip a piece of paper under his pillow but didn't think anything of it. She propped the door open and walked to his side.

"Good evening, Mr. Carson. We might be able to take those stitches out today."

"I hope so. I'll have you know I almost took them out myself. *But* I showed some restraint, and they're still there."

His words were teasing but he didn't smile. Kate thought it was a little odd, but she shrugged it off.

As she prepared her supplies, she changed her voice to one of mock gravity. "That is quite an accomplishment. Thank you for listening to me."

"You're welcome, Miss Morrison." He nodded and gave her a little grin.

"What? No Miss Kit?" she teased. He seemed a little different and she wanted to help him feel better.

Boone looked at her with a hint of uncertainty in his eyes. "You...you'd let me call you that?"

"Well, no. But I might relent and let you call me Miss Kate instead." She shrugged her shoulders playfully and Boone gave a weak smile.

"I suppose that's progress."

"It is. Call it a reward for being a good patient." She paused and looked at him. "Well, mostly good," she said with a smile.

He chuckled at her teasing and seemed to relax a little more, so Kate started her routine of checking his wound.

She brought the oil lamp closer and placed a clean towel under his leg before taking off the bandages. As she cleaned the area with warm water, she saw that the wound still looked unpleasant, but the skin had closed well enough for the stitches to come out.

She looked up and saw Boone staring across the room, but he looked at her once her fingers stopped moving. "Once these are out, the wound still needs to finish healing without the stitches."

"You're the doc." Boone's voice betrayed his growing excitement for the news.

"So," she said, wagging her finger at him, "if you put too much strain on the injury, it will split open again and I will make you start the whole process over." She patted her bag as a mock threat. "Don't tempt me to stab you with that needle again."

Boone held his hands up in surrender. "I promise to be extra careful till my bizarre doctor says so."

"Marvelous." She grabbed her scissors and tweezers. "Now hold still and this will go quickly." She leaned close to his leg and got to work.

The pair sat in silence as she worked. Normally, Boone would be chatting by now and Kate wondered if something was wrong. She debated whether she should ask him about it. Once the first stitch was removed though, he began talking.

"What is your opinion about...about arranged marriages?"

Kate's hands went still.

Boone watched Kate's hands stop moving and lips pinch and knew instantly she had a strong opinion about it.

He'd asked about the progress on the arrangement in his letter home informing his family of his delayed arrival. Boone had just received his mama's response earlier that day and its contents were weighing heavily on his mind.

. . . You must not have gotten my earlier letter, but we found a suitable match. Her family, the Kingstons, are wealthy and well known in Roseburg, Oregon. They have an excellent reputation, and we have been in constant correspondence since making the arrangement. They look forward to meeting you and are excited for you to marry their daughter. Come home as soon as you are able. I sincerely hope this meets with your approval.

I love you always, son. Be safe. Love, Mama

P.S. Her name is Katarina. Isn't that pretty?

Technically, his mama had done exactly what Boone asked, but for some reason, he wasn't sure he still wanted that. He'd been stewing over it when Kate had arrived, and he wanted to know what she thought. In fact, he wanted to know what she thought about many things—about everything.

"So?" He was almost afraid to know the answer. For some reason, he felt like he was disappointing her.

Kate turned to him, her eyes wide and lips tight.

"Is this the one and only time I ask you something and you have nothing to say?" Boone teased, trying to dispel some of the tension.

She turned back to his stitches. "Well, what am I supposed to say about such a question?"

"Answer honestly?"

She snipped another stitch then paused to look at him. "Answer honestly? Fine. I think they are abhorrent." She turned back to her task and pulled the thread out with very little gentleness, making Boone flinch. "Sorry," came her remorseless reply.

"I knew you'd have an opinion. I just didn't realize it would be so strong," he said, sitting back.

"Why shouldn't it be? I hardly think we need something so archaic in our society."

"Why not? It works for some people," Boone said, trying to prod her for more. He admired her unusual independent spirit and he wanted to know her mind.

Kate exhaled sharply and placed her scissors and tweezers on the towel before turning to face him. Boone enjoyed the moments when he had her full attention but, instinctively, he knew this would not be like the light-hearted debates they'd enjoyed before.

"It might work for people who actually want it. But what about the people who don't want an arrangement, but are forced into it?"

"I would say that they both have terrible parents."

He was unprepared for the breathy smile she gave him in response. It only lasted a moment, but she seemed relieved about something.

"Let me ask you this then," Kate said.

Boone nodded and leaned closer.

"What if an arrangement is proposed? One person agrees with it and genuinely wants it but the other..." she paused, "...the other person does not. What should happen then?"

Boone thought for a moment. "I'd say the arrangement shouldn't happen. If it does, the couple would be miserable for the rest of their lives."

"Precisely my thoughts. But how would you know if one person did not want to go through with it?"

Her question confused Boone. "You would ask them?" Boone thought it was the most obvious answer, but Kate shook her head.

"That's not always possible, especially if the parents are in control of the arrangement. They might do anything to silence their children."

Boone watched Kate's eyes and for one brief second, he noticed a flash of pain in their chocolatey depths. This conversation had clearly pulled up difficult memories for her. He wished she would expound on her thoughts, but just like the other times he'd asked her about her life before Brexton, she avoided telling him. He knew she was keeping things from him. He wanted to respect her privacy, but he also wished she trusted him.

"So, in your opinion," Boone said, "when is an arranged marriage permitted?"

"I guess...if both parties seek for and agree to it and hold to that agreement, then I don't see why it should be a problem. If an arranged marriage is requested and accepted, it should be treated the same as a promise. And...," she pointed her finger at him, "people should never break a promise."

Boone said nothing but nodded. He wanted to know more about what was behind her response to his question, but he knew this was not the time to discover it.

"Why did you ask me that?" Kate said, picking up her tools again. Her movements were stiff and jerky.

Boone panicked slightly. "Oh. My...uh...mama told me about a friend back home whose parents arranged his marriage for him. I guess it was just fresh on my mind."

Kate paused and considered him for a moment. Eventually, she shrugged and turned back to her task of removing his stitches. They fell into easy conversation, though his mind wasn't fully focused on it.

He felt uncertain about his own circumstances and decided he wouldn't tell Kate anything until he'd learned a little more about his arrangement. As soon as she left his room, he planned to write to his mama.

Secretly, he hoped the unknown woman in Oregon didn't want their arrangement at all. Secretly, he wanted to see what might blossom between him and Kate.

Not so secretly, he liked her beauty, compassion, and fire.

Eight

A few days had passed since Kate had removed Boone's stitches. Both he and Jesse were showing vast improvements with their health and spirits since they arrived in Brexton, and they each credited it to the attention they were getting from Kate and Beth, respectively. Charlotte's excellent cooking was also a big factor.

Although her clientele was growing, Kate still found herself struggling to balance her time as a seamstress and her time caring for Boone. She hadn't begun fixing the shop as her landlord originally requested and the guilt was starting the weigh on her. However, Kate felt the delicate dance was worth it because of her budding friendship with Boone.

But her delight was dampened as Mr. Dixon insisted on frequenting her shop, always asking her to spend less time with Boone and more time with him. One time he went as far as to say he was thinking about getting hurt just to get her attention, though he had laughed it off like some bad joke. She found every encounter disagreeable, but never mentioned her experiences to anyone else.

She was still astonished the town shared Charlotte's opinion and considered him to be an amiable and well-liked man. She knew he'd arrived in Brexton shortly after she did, and the town had quickly welcomed him. Despite his rough appearance, he was always ready to help his "fellow neighbors". This just added to her dislike of the man since Brexton had accepted him so quickly, while she had to prove herself worthy of the town's trust.

Beth related many stories of Mr. Dixon's contributions to the town and how he was always friendly and boisterous to everyone who spoke to him. Beth had babbled on about him buying peppermint every week and giving it to children. He'd even shared some with her with a wink and a compliment.

As much as Kate had tried to see Mr. Dixon through Beth's eyes, she saw only a hint of a respectable man when other people were around. Whenever they were alone, Kate always felt the overpowering urge to use lye and boiling water to scrub her skin raw.

Kate mulled over this as she walked to the boarding house for lunch.

When Kate entered the house, she inhaled the enticing smell wafting from the kitchen. She looked over to Boone's bedroom door and wanted to go straight there, but the smell proved to be too tempting and she walked into the dining room first. Greeting the few guests already at the table, she entered the kitchen.

"Charlotte, this smells wonderful. Do you need any help?"

"Never you mind. I have everythin' under control. How're things at your shop?" She said, stirring the beef stew.

"It is starting to pick up." Kate sank onto a stool at the counter.

"Well, you're immensely popular now with all the women around town. They fawn over your designs. And I gotta say the men folk are appreciative as well," Charlotte said, wiggling her eyebrows.

Kate sighed gratefully and gave a small smile. "That's wonderful to hear. But with everything I have in the shop, I'm finding it difficult to stay organized. There is still so much work to be done." She leaned forward, resting her head in her hands. "I want to provide my best for everyone, but it takes too long to dig through my supplies that have no permanent home yet. Besides, I don't have the money or skills to build the shelves I have been wanting."

A sly grin pulled at the corners of Charlotte's mouth. "I see. I'm sure we can do somethin' about that."

"I know. I will just wait and work on my organizational skills."

"In the meantime, though, will you go bring back Jesse and Boone? Lunch is ready and I'm sure they're chomping at the bit for somethin' to eat."

Kate looked at Charlotte. "What is Mr. Carson doing out back? He should still be resting." Kate jumped to her feet and left through the back door. As soon as she was outside, she noticed Boone splitting logs by the barn, his back to her.

"And just what do you think you are doing?" Kate asked, marching toward him, hands on her hips.

He turned his head and smiled. "I'm cutting some wood for Miss Charlotte. She said it needed to be done, and Jesse took off for a bit with Beth. I figured I could help instead of being a lazy lump on a log." He chuckled when she crossed her arms and gave him a stern look. "I'm fine, Kit. I know my limits," Boone said, turning his head from her and lifting the axe over his head once more, bringing it down in a smooth motion.

"I am the one who says when you are ready to do physical labor, Mr. Carson. And would you stop calling me Kit? My name is Kate," she said.

Boone sighed and turned about. Kate's gaze was immediately drawn to his shirt, three buttons undone. She could see he wore no undershirt, leaving a clear view of his lean but well-sculpted chest. She averted her gaze and felt her face flush.

"As you keep saying." She heard him chuckle—presumably at her discomfort.

Kate shook her head but kept her eyes down. "How is your leg feeling today?"

"Same as yesterday. Just a bit stiff and sore, but I need to do something or I'm gonna go crazy," Boone said.

She glanced at him and she saw him fasten two buttons, leaving the last one open. His eyes met hers and a torrent of butterflies filled her stomach. She began to relax a little—but only a little

"I should...I should go find Jesse." She ducked past him.

"Running off so soon, Kit? Jesse's with Beth on a picnic." Kate could hear the smile in his voice, and she turned to see his eyes dance. Her heart leapt to her throat and she swallowed hard.

"Shall we go inside then?" She looked at the clump of dirt by her shoe and focused on that.

"I can't say no to Miss Charlotte's wonderful cooking," he said, slapping his stomach. "Though it might not do my figure any good. What do you think?"

Kate put a hand to her cheek to try and hide her blush as she walked past him again. "I think you will be just fine. Though you are slightly on the thin side if you ask me."

The low cadence of Boone's laugh rumbled through Kate. "Thanks. I'll work on that."

Boone came up beside her. "How is the shop going?"

Kate was relieved he changed the subject. "I am still trying to get things organized, but people seem to be happy with my work, so I can figure the rest of it out later." Kate said, walking slow to accommodate Boone's pronounced limp.

"What needs to be done to help with the organization?" Boone asked, holding the back kitchen door open.

She nodded in thanks as she passed through the door. "Well, most of the shelves left from the previous tenant are too small or need repairs, and my worktable is too small for what I need. I cannot afford to hire someone to build some yet, but I might take them apart myself."

"What're you two talkin' about?" Charlotte asked, walking into the kitchen from the dining room and grabbing the last few bowls of stew.

"Kate was just telling me she needed some help in her shop with some woodworking." Boone took one of the bowls from Charlotte and placed a quick peck on her cheek. Kate thought it was sweet how they had taken to one another. Charlotte had certainly looked out for him like he was her own son.

"And how is the most beautiful woman in Brexton?" Boone asked, dipping his finger into the uncooked cake batter on the counter.

"Boone Carson, you keep your fingers out of there. That's for dessert tonight." Charlotte wagged her finger at him as he smiled and ducked toward the dining room while licking the chocolate off his fingers.

Kate and Charlotte chuckled and followed Boone into where the other patrons were already eating.

Boone pulled chairs out for the ladies before sitting down next to Kate and scooping some stew into his mouth. "Miss Charlotte, you've outdone yourself again. I swear I'm feeling better every day." Boone said around a mouth full of food. Charlotte smiled at him like only mothers do and accepted the compliment.

"But," he continued, "now I need you to put me to work. Hard work. Not just chopping some firewood. If I'm gonna be here till the end of June, I need to earn my keep. Besides, I don't want your cooking to turn me into a dumpling." Everyone at the table chuckled. Kate was sure he hadn't resembled a dumpling since his infancy.

Charlotte thought for a moment. "Mr. Carson, I have no grand projects I need you to do but," she looked at Kate mischievously, "why don't you help Miss Morrison fix her shop?"

Kate's mouth dropped in astonishment.

Boone, however, beamed. "What an excellent idea, Miss Charlotte." He turned to Kate then. "What do you say, Miss Kit?"

Kate gawked at him. "Mr. Carson, I...I don't know what to say."

"Say you'll accept my help," he said, extending his hand for her to shake. Kate stared at it, her eyes wide.

"I cannot pay you for the work. It would not feel right."

"You've given me my life and let me keep my leg. I would say I'm in your debt. And anyways, it's fine to accept help when it's being offered."

Kate looked at Charlotte and the other tenants for help. "What about propriety?"

A gentleman across from Kate cleared his throat. "I don't see why that would be inappropriate. Your shop is far more public than your bedside nursing, Miss. No one will look down on you for having a handyman around."

Charlotte nodded in agreement.

"Most of the work will be done outside anyway," Boone said, nodding his appreciation to the gentleman.

Looking at Boone now, Kate noticed how much healthier—not to mention how much more attractive—he looked. Boone kept his facial hair shaved but often sported a day or two's whisker growth, which just made him more handsome. He boasted a square jawline and a small but very appealing cleft in his chin, both framed by his long dark hair. It was thick, and she noticed that he often ran his fingers through it. Despite being bedridden, he had changed from sickly and gaunt to healthy and handsome. Every day, his eyes gained more of a twinkle of mischief and merriment, and Kate found herself in a constant struggle to avoid getting lost in them. Now, the only outward effect from the war was his limp, although she noticed he had taken great care to hide it as he walked.

"He will be a distraction," Kate said, her voice low and distant. Boone only chuckled and ate some more stew.

"I think that's a small price to pay for the help Boone is offerin' ya," Charlotte said, giving Kate a knowing smile.

Kate wished she could stop blushing. She attempted to appear unflustered, even though she felt like she'd just been caught contemplating Boone's good looks.

"If you reopen the hole in your leg, all my work and all your waiting will be wasted," she said.

Boone put a hand to his chest in mock excitement. "Oh, Miss Kit, ya do care for me," he said. Sarcasm dripped from every word, but Kate felt the truth of them. When had she started to care so much for him? He winked at her and a warmth flooded her heart. The prospect of still being able to see him often made her feel nervous and excited all at once.

"It's a deal then," she said as she stuck out her hand. Boone took it and shook firmly.

"I'll be by later to take some measurements," he said. Kate released his hand and looked down at her half-eaten lunch, her heart thundering in her chest.

What did I just agree to?

Nine

Boone hadn't gotten the chance to see Brexton due to his injury, and he enjoyed his exploration. His leg still ached when he moved, but he was walking. It was better than staying cooped up in one room for ten days. He found Brexton quaint but still filled with life. At any given moment, he could fall into easy conversation with another person, and he craved being more social than he'd been able to be back home.

Now that he'd familiarized himself with the town, Boone focused on finding the post office since he had a letter to send to his mama before heading to Kate's shop. After his conversation with Kate about arranged marriages, he'd written his thoughts in the letter and was determined to send it.

Through their interactions, Boone quickly learned that he liked talking with Kate. He felt as though she was waking him up from the darkness of the war and helping him find himself again. He'd reevaluated his capability of having a proper courtship, and he knew he could easily do so if it was with Kate. Though it was still too soon to know exactly what was happening between them, Boone knew he wanted to find out.

But Kate's words and convictions about breaking promises caused him to wonder if she would look on him kindly if he fled the arrangement he had requested. He had to know whether the woman possibly waiting for him back home actually wanted this or whether she'd been coerced.

He clutched the letter tightly in his hand and hoped his mama wouldn't think he'd gone mad in the desert once she read his words.

Dear Mama and Pa,
My leg is healing fine. There's a young
woman at the boarding house where I'm
staying that has fine medical training and has
been caring for my wound. She is unique in
some of her methods, but I have to admit
that they yield quick results. She took my
stitches out only moments ago, and our re-
cent conversation is why I'm writing you.

I asked what her opinion was about arranged
marriages, and she told me—quite strongly,
I might add. But there was something she
mentioned that I needed to ask you about as
soon as possible. Did Miss Kingston agree to
this arrangement? If she doesn't want this,
I have no wish to force her. In fact, I'm
starting to think that I might not want to go
through with it myself. I know what I said in

*my original request, but there is something
I'd like to see about here in Brexton before I
make a final decision.*

*I apologize for the confusion I've no doubt
caused. Send everyone my love.
Boone*

After dropping it off to be delivered, Boone couldn't stop the smile spreading across his face as he made his way toward Kate's shop. She had told him so much about it, and he knew she was proud of it, even with all the work that still needed to be done. He admired her independence.

His excitement grew as the shop came into view, and though his leg was aching a bit, he pushed the pain aside. The little bell tinkled as he pushed the door open. He hoped his arrival would put a smile on her face, but any hope of that faded quickly once he realized what was happening inside.

A burly man stood only inches from Kate, his great grubby hands on her waist. The look on Kate's face told Boone that this was not a welcome invasion of her personal space. Fire rained in Boone's veins, and he limped across the shop to stand directly behind them. "Get your hands off her!" he growled. The stench of tobacco filled the space around them.

The large man slowly took his hands off Kate and turned around, an easy smile spread across his face. "This ain't none of yer business. Kindly keep walkin'." The lazy droll of the man's words were emphasized by the tilt of his head toward Boone.

"That may be true, but it doesn't look like she'd like you to stay, so I suggest you leave." Boone's hands were balled.

A hint of a sneer peeked through the man's smile. "I don't think we've officially met mister, so I'm thinkin' maybe you shouldn't interrupt the pleasant conversation between me and the lady." He stepped closer to Kate and grabbed her hand.

"I can speak for myself," she said, yanking her hand out of the foul man's grasp and taking a few steps away.

"Hear that? She doesn't want you around, so move along," Boone said.

"I didn't hear those words from her," Dixon said, getting in Boone's face. The man was confident, his sneer fully evident now. Boone stood straight and returned the scowl.

"Leave. Both of you," Kate said. "I have work to do and I don't have time for this. Please."

Boone glanced over to Kate and saw the pleading in her eyes. Looking back to the large man, he wasn't convinced the brute would listen to Kate's plea. But he scoffed in Boone's face and soon, the same easy smile spread across his face as he stepped around Boone.

"See, Miss Kate? When ya ask nice, anythin' could happen." He sent a smile to Kate that made Boone uneasy and walked out of the shop, leaving his stench behind.

Boone wondered if others could see how two-faced this man really was. He also wondered why Kate put up with it.

Kate stood by her table; her hand braced against the edge. "I believe I asked both of you to leave."

Boone didn't say anything. He watched as she smoothed the fabric of her dress and closed her eyes for a moment, her chest rising and falling slowly. When she opened her eyes again, she cleared her throat.

"I'm sorry. I didn't mean to snap at you." She forced a bright smile that didn't reach her eyes. "What can I do for you, Mr. Carson?" She started taking a few things off the shelves.

Boone rubbed his leg, sore from his long walk. "I'm here to take some measurements. But that doesn't matter right now."

Kate looked away.

Boone moved closer. "He may have tried to seem innocent, but that man doesn't have honorable intentions toward you. And if he's that same man I heard from outside my door, it looks like he's been that way for a while."

Kate stared intently at her shoes but said nothing.

"What's his name?"

Kate looked up at him for a moment, and Boone could see her debating whether she should tell him. Finally, she closed her eyes and shook her head. "His name is Lez Dixon."

Boone took another step forward. "Why haven't you told anyone about this? We've talked a lot. Why didn't you tell me? Or Charlotte? Or Beth? The last time I asked, you said he was just a customer, but that's obviously not true."

Kate shook her head. "I have dealt with him this long, and I can continue."

"How long?"

Her head snapped up. "I don't owe you any information, Mr. Carson. I am perfectly capable of taking care of myself and my shop. I don't require yours or anyone else's help."

Boone saw the fire in her eyes, but it was mingled with fear. While he admired her determination, he wished she would let him in. He didn't know the specifics of the situation, but he could guess, and that guess made him want to string the charlatan up.

Boone sighed, knowing he had to be careful. "I've no doubt you have the drive to accomplish anything you wish. But you should know that you don't have to do it alone." He took another step closer. "You have people who will help you." He hoped she understood.

Kate just stared at him before nodding feebly.

"Good. Now, can I sit for a spell? I made a promise to some crazy lady doctor that I wouldn't overstrain my leg." His words produced the desired effect, and Kate gave him a small smile that finally reached her eyes.

Boone sat with her for a little while, listening to her talk about her shop as she worked on her various projects. He liked watching her hands move deftly across the fabrics.

She didn't mention anything regarding Dixon again, and Boone didn't press her. But he could tell that the man wasn't going to back down. Boone suspected that he would start to increase his advances, and Boone's protective nature flared. He would have to watch out for Kate, regardless of her pride.

Ten

Kate couldn't believe all the progress Boone had made in the past few days. The two tables he'd worked on looked like new, and the shelf he built was such a blessing to her workspace that she couldn't believe how much of a difference it made for her.

He'd also been walking her to and from work every day, which gave them more time to talk and get to know each other. Since he was up and moving, his mood had improved by leaps and bounds. He laughed more and was always the first to help Charlotte with the dishes. But once he started working, she had a tough time focusing on her own work.

Today was no different. Boone had walked her to the shop and begun working at the back. She'd had to run to the general store while she didn't have customers. As Kate made her way back down the boardwalk, she could hear the methodical knock of his hammer. Several people waved or smiled as she passed, and she was grateful for their warm greetings.

Her door was almost in sight, but she froze in place as she saw Mr. Dixon. The shadowy form of the hefty man loomed in the street before her, his broad shoulders and booming voice giving him away. He was helping a young family load their wagon with a few supplies from the farrier. The sound of their laugher reached her ears, and the woman was smiling appreciatively at him. Kate's stomach rolled in knots.

Why was he awful only to me?

Ducking her head, she hurried along, boots clicking rapidly on the boardwalk. She reached her door and flung it open, her heart pounding in her chest as she slumped to the floor. She took several calming breaths. Once her heart had slowed, she got to her feet and placed the items she'd purchased on the table. She ran her fingers down the soft bristles of the scrub brush she'd bought.

The quiet tinkle of the bell alerted her to someone's arrival, and she turned to see who it was. Her stomach dropped.

Mr. Dixon.

Kate braced herself for the onslaught she knew was coming.

"Good afternoon, Miss Morrison," he said, tipping his hat.

"Is there something you need, sir?" She didn't try to sound cheerful. Her patience was wearing thin trying to put up with the likes of him.

"I just came by to see ya. No need to get snippy." He sauntered over, and Kate was glad that she was standing behind the counter.

"I am a busy woman, Mr. Dixon. If you need nothing today, move along." She gestured to the door. She looked at the back door through which she could hear the pound of a hammer.

He narrowed his eyes and scowled, leaning toward her over the counter. "Havin' this man workin' here has people talkin'. It ain't right to have an unmarried woman spendin' so much time with a man she don't know."

"Whom I ask for help in my store is none of your concern, Mr. Dixon." Kate straightened her back.

"I say it does!" In a flurry of movement, Mr. Dixon reached across the counter and grabbed her upper arms, and pulled her towards him. With his face only inches away from her own, the potent reek of tobacco hit Kate's nose and the distinct urge to vomit nearly overwhelmed her. She struggled to free herself, but he had both her arms pinned to her side.

"I gotta admit, I'm gettin' tired of these little games. Ya know I have intentions toward ya," he said, pulling her closer and rubbing his cheek over hers. She heard a long inhale and realized he was sniffing her hair. Her hands were still free and she pushed her palms against the edge of the counter with all her might even though the action seemed useless.

"Hmmm, ya sure smell nice." He pulled back and looked at her mouth. He licked his lips and leaned toward her, but she thrashed her head from side to side, trying to avoid his repugnant mouth.

"Don't touch me!" Mr. Dixon's grip loosened slightly and Kate ripped herself from his grasp. The force of it had her stumbling backward.

"Now, Kate." He stepped around the counter. She backed away as his hand reached for her once more, the golden ring on his finger winked in the light.

Suddenly, someone came rushing from behind her and pushed Mr. Dixon. The large man grunted, lost his footing, and slumped to the floor.

"Boone!" Relief flooded Kate as Boone put his body between her and her attacker. Taking her arms softly, he pulled her to him in a protective embrace. Her hands clung to his shirt, and she buried her face in his shoulder.

"What do you think you're doing, you lowlife?" Boone said, his voice echoing around the small room. Kate turned her face to look at Boone. Though he was holding her, he never took his eyes off of Mr. Dixon, who had lumbered to his feet again.

"Boy, I've had about enough of yer meddlin' in my business," Mr. Dixon grumbled, pointing a menacing finger at Boone.

"I don't much care what you've had enough of. Though I would say you're the unwelcome one meddling in Kate's life." Boone looked from her to Mr. Dixon. She nodded her head, not missing the way Mr. Dixon's hands balled into fists.

"I weren't askin' boy! Move along!" Dixon shouted, lunging toward them. Boone pushed Kate out of the way, avoiding the arcing blow. In the next moment, he caught Mr. Dixon's hand and deftly twisted it up and behind his back. He yelped in pain as Boone forced him into a deeper armlock.

"You are no longer welcome here," Kate said as Boone maneuvered Mr. Dixon to a standing position. With both of them upright, she could see that Boone was a few inches taller and had thick muscles roping down his arms. Mr. Dixon was wider, but Boone had no trouble directing him toward the door. Kate moved swiftly and opened it. "And I intend to speak to the sheriff about this."

Mr. Dixon strained his neck to look from Kate to Boone. "Ol' Sheriff Garrett? I only seen him once since I got here, and that was a mighty friendly conversation."

He gave her a malicious smile that shriveled her insides. "Sheriff Garrett is too old to help ya, and yer pretty boy won't be around all the time." At that, Boone pushed Mr. Dixon's arm up, making him twist and holler. As Boone held him and moved him closer to the door, he protested loudly, spewing profanities and threats toward both Kate and Boone. Again, Kate thought, *How do people not see this man for who he is?*

Finally at the doorway, Boone shoved an angry Mr. Dixon through. Kate followed them out, intending to stay close to Boone. Several of the townspeople stopped in the street as they passed.

Reaching the edge of the boardwalk, Mr. Dixon struggled again. His movements caused both men to lose their footing, and they tumbled into the street. Mr. Dixon landed hard on Boone's legs.

Kate watched in horror as both men scrambled up from their fall. Mr. Dixon recovered first and lunged at Boone with a raised fist. Kate screamed a warning too late, and Dixon slammed his fist into Boone's jaw. Boone stumbled back, dazed and off-balance, but he regained his footing. Mr. Dixon pulled a knife from his boot and taunted Boone with it.

"I got ya figured out, boy. Yer sweet on Kate, and yer mad she prefers me," Dixon sneered under his breath. "In fact, yer mad that I got my hands on her first. She sure is soft." Kate's stomach rolled at his words.

With a shout, Boone bent at the waist and charged toward Mr. Dixon's extensive midsection, knocking him over. As he did, Boone roared in anger or pain—Kate couldn't tell. Then he was on top of Mr. Dixon, his fists flying. Kate rushed toward Boone, trying to pull him away.

"Stop! That is enough. Let's just go." She pulled again on Boone's shirt, but he just ignored her.

The fighting had attracted the attention of the townsfolk, who were now watching the brawl in disgust. Kate overheard two women talking nearby. "I can't believe this. That soldier is attacking sweet Mr. Dixon."

"Such disgraceful behavior," the woman's companion said.

Kate's jaw dropped in bewilderment. *They really have no idea who this man is.* She shook her head as she continued to watch the brutal scene unfold before her.

Boone scrambled to his feet and grabbed Mr. Dixon's collar, pulling him up just enough to slam his face into a solid knee. Kate heard the distinct crack of a nose breaking, and a shiver ran up her spine at the blood running from Mr. Dixon's nose. He dropped his knife as both hands flew to his face.

"You broke my nose!" he shouted, one hand wiping the blood from his face onto his pants.

"You deserve far more than a broken nose after what you've done. And I mean to give it to you." Boone moved as if to hit him again.

Before he reached Mr. Dixon, Kate rushed forward and grabbed his arm, halting his attack. "Boone, enough. Stop!"

Boone looked from her to Mr. Dixon, who was curled up on the ground. She pulled at Boone's arm again, and he lowered it before turning and limping away. Two men helped Mr. Dixon sit up, but both glared at Boone while Kate lead him away from the street.

Clutching his arm, Kate pulled Boone to sit on the bench in front of her shop. He groaned as he fell onto the seat and went on to inspect his torn-up knuckles. Kate tried to calm the pounding of her heart. Seeing Boone in pain had been difficult for her, but now she needed to be a nurse again. Among the various welts, bruises, and cuts, there was a gash on his left shoulder. She assumed it was from Mr. Dixon's knife, but she couldn't remember seeing him inflict the wound.

After running into her shop for a few rags, she brought them to Boone and began to apply pressure to the laceration. "I thought we had a deal that you wouldn't get yourself hurt," she said, applying pressure to the wound.

The muscles in his shoulder tensed. "Technically, I didn't break the deal. I sustained these injuries outside of your shop."

She rolled her eyes as he chuckled at his own wit.

"Let's get you home and patched up," Kate said, looping his right arm around her shoulders. He was heavier than she expected.

"What's going on here?" asked an authoritative voice that boomed around the square.

"He attacked me, Sheriff." Mr. Dixon raised his bloodied hand toward Boone while being lifted to his feet by the other men.

"Not before you harassed Miss Morrison," Boone said, narrowing his eyes at Mr. Dixon.

"Is this true, Miss Morrison?" The sheriff turned to look at Kate.

"I...well..." Kate looked down at the dirt. She hated having everyone look at her, and she doubted that they would believe what actually happened.

"Miss Morrison?"

She searched the townspeople's faces for some sign of what to do, but most of them just looked horrified at what they were hearing—not to mention what they had seen happen between Boone and Mr. Dixon. The rest of the people who had gathered seemed curious as to what she would say about their beloved neighbor.

The sheriff moved forward. "Shall we talk somewhere more private?"

Kate nodded, relieved.

"Fine. Let's go talk in my office and—"

Kate interrupted him. "I should get Mr. Carson to the boarding house. Once I tend to his injuries, I can come find you?" She could feel her stomach twist at the thought of retelling what had happened. *Perhaps the sheriff would believe me.*

"Why not take him to Doc Jones?" the sheriff asked. "He just got back."

Kate looked over to the two men who were half supporting, half dragging a bloodied Mr. Dixon toward Doc Jones's clinic that was just down the dusty street to her left. The sheriff followed her gaze and nodded when he understood her hesitation.

"I'll stop by the boarding house in an hour."

Kate nodded and Boone groaned. Sheriff Garrett shooed the remaining crowd away. The breath Kate had been holding left her in a rush. She could feel Boone's eyes on her, but she wasn't about to say anything more.

"Let's get you home." Together they made slow progress toward the boarding house, his limp becoming more pronounced with each step.

Once they finally got to the side door by the kitchen, Kate looked at Boone, unsure of what she should say.

"Were you ever going to say anything to anyone about what was going on with Dixon?" Boone asked as he slipped onto one of the chairs at the table. His eyes had grown serious.

"I would have eventually." She pulled back his shirt from his shoulder and focused on the wound. It didn't seem to be too deep of a gash, but she would have to thoroughly clean it, and Boone wasn't going to like it. "But I can take care of myself." She motioned for him to take off his shirt. Luckily, his undershirt was intact and was only stained with a little blood. She grabbed the water pitcher and soap.

"Kit, you don't need to do everything on your own."

"But I do." She grabbed the shirt out of his hands and pressed hard on his shoulder.

He withdrew from her touch, wincing. "Dang, if I didn't know you were so good at this doctoring stuff, I would say you were trying to hurt me." He eased back toward her, and she continued to clean the wound. "You have wonderful friends here. Let them help you."

"Charlotte has enough on her plate with this place," Kate said, tilting her head toward the rest of the boarding house. "And Beth has the wedding to plan and Jesse to look after—you two are quite the pair actually. From what Beth tells me, he was always getting into trouble, but he doesn't seem to need all the stitching and bandaging that you do.

"I'm a hardworking man, and I got the scars to prove it," he said, lifting his undershirt to point to a scar on his abdomen. "See this one? Got that from flying off a horse into a fence—my family was well known for the horses we sold. I broke that brute three days later." The scar was long and jagged Kate could only imagine the time it would have taken to stitch him back together, and she couldn't imagine the pain he would have endured from the injury while breaking a horse.

"And this one." He lifted the shirt further and moved his fingers to the left side of his chest. "Got that one from fighting with my younger brother. He was mad I made him muck out the barn for the third day in a row."

"Seems to me that you have more scars from being reckless than from being hard working," she said, heat filling her face as her attention was pulled to his muscular torso. He was making it difficult for her to concentrate on the task at hand. Realizing she was staring at his chest, she snapped her attention back to the shoulder wound and tried to appear busy. Out of the corner of her eye, she saw him smile triumphantly. She couldn't help but smile sheepishly as she shook her head.

Using a new rag, she soaped up the gash and started to scrub it clean. She glanced at Boone and almost laughed at his concentrated grimace—he was obviously trying to appear unaffected.

"I'm sorry," she said. "I'm almost done." She didn't like putting him through more pain, even if it was necessary.

"I didn't really feel it when he cut me during our scuffle, but I sure feel it now. Are you sure you're not trying to scrub my shoulder off?"

Kate looked at him, bewildered. "How did you not realize that you had been cut so badly?" She started applying a loose bandage.

He shrugged his good shoulder. "I dunno. He landed on my bad leg before that, and that hurt worse." Her eyes drifted to the where the wound on his leg was healing. Nothing seemed amiss externally, so she refocused on his shoulder.

"You know, Charlotte is going to have my head when she sees what happened to you," Kate said as she finished wrapping a clean bandage around his battered shoulder.

"It might be sooner than you think," Boone said. His eyes had locked onto something behind Kate.

"My goodness, what's happened to you now, Boone?" The motherly tone of Charlotte's voice poked the guilt Kate already felt. She knew Charlotte had lost all but one of her children, though she didn't know how. But in the short amount of time Boone had been there, it seemed that Charlotte had taken him in as one of her own.

"Nothing serious, Mrs. Conrad. Just a little tussle." Boone stood to greet Charlotte.

Jesse's voice echoed from the parlor. "Lez Dixon, of all people. Why on earth would you pick a fight with him? By all accounts, he's a friendly and helpful man." Jesse's figure appeared in the kitchen doorway.

"Yes, Kate. Of all the people in town, why did I pick a fight with Lez Dixon?" Boone looked pointedly at Kate.

"What does Kate have to do with you gettin' in a fight?" Charlotte asked. Kate could feel all the eyes in the room look to her. She wanted to hide under a mountain.

Eleven

"How long has this been going on Miss Morrison?" The sheriff's voice was low but gruff.

She hung her head. "I...well...," she said, her eyes slipping closed. They still sat in the kitchen of the boarding house. Jesse, Boone, and Charlotte stood to one side, while Kate and Sheriff Garrett sat at the table.

"How long, Miss?"

"It wasn't this bad, I promise." Her eyes stung with frustrated tears. "But once I got the shop and Boone arrived, he became...," she took a shaky breath, "more persistent."

"How long?"

There was no avoiding it. "The same day he arrived—only a day or two after I had arrived myself."

Boone heaved a deep breath before pulling a chair out next to her and sliding into it. He took her hand and gently held it between his. She felt the hot tears slide down her cheeks unbidden but didn't wipe them away.

"I asked Beth about Mr. Dixon once." Kate looked at the empty space between the people in the room, refusing to look at any of them. "She said not much was known about him, but everyone seemed to like him. He was a decent-looking single man. Respectful and kind and always had candy in his pockets for children. He was always willing to help. With a reputation like that, who would have believed me? I am a single woman traveling alone. I had to work so hard just to have people say hello to me in the street." She looked directly at the sheriff. There was talk among the people in town that he didn't take women seriously—especially unmarried ones.

"Doesn't matter," Boone said. "You should be able to live and work in peace without being treated disrespectfully."

"I was handling him just fine until you came around." She pulled her hand back and folded her arms. "If you didn't try to provoke him every time you saw him, things might have never escalated."

"Kit." Boone's voice was low, and she turned back to face him. Staring at her, his eyes filled with an odd expression she couldn't identify, but it sent a flurry of tingles down her spine. He opened his mouth to say something, then stopped himself and shook his head. "Never mind," he said finally, running his hand through his hair. Kate knew that what she'd said had been unkind, and the hard press of Boone's lips combined with the narrowing of his eyes only served to further her guilt.

"Please, Miss Morrison, explain more," Sheriff Garrett said.

Kate sighed. "At first it was lewd and insinuative comments. I thought he was harmless. But lately..." Kate could feel her throat burning with tension, "I always asked him to leave. I never gave him any idea that I had any interest in him, but he seems to think that I did." She covered her face in her hands.

"He backed her into a corner and wasn't letting her go. And that wasn't the first time he's put his hands on her," Boone said.

"Mr. Carson, if I have any questions for ya, I'll ask. But you addin' your..." Sheriff Garrett waved his hand in the air, "*embellishments* doesn't help. From what Miss Morrison said, he was just trying to get a young lady's attention. No harm in that." He finished with a stern look.

Kate looked from the sheriff to Charlotte, whose eyes were searching Kate's face. She hoped that the older woman was trying to figure out what had really happened. Charlotte opened her mouth as if to speak.

Kate lifted her hand to stop her. "I'm fine," she said, taking a deep breath.

The sheriff continued. "From what you've said, Miss. Morrison, I'm sorry to inform you that there ain't enough evidence for me to take any immediate action against him. But I'll tell you that I've had my eye on him since his arrival, like all new arrivals, and I haven't found anythin' untoward in his behavior. I'll take what you've told me into consideration, but I have more pressin' matters to deal with." He grabbed his hat and stood. "And Mr. Carson, I must advise you not to attack him again. It will not warm you to this town. Be careful." His dark eyes glared at Boone.

"So that's it then? You're not going to do anything for Kate?" Boone jumped to his feet.

But the sheriff only rolled his eyes. "Watch yourself, Mr. Carson or I'll have you stay a night in jail. Perhaps that will teach you to control your temper." With that, he thanked Charlotte and left.

Kate dropped her hands into her lap and let the rest of her tears slip down her cheeks.

"I believe you, Kate." Charlotte placed her hand on Kate's shoulder, her comforting touch soothing some of Kate's fears.

"Thank you." She patted Charlotte's hand.

"Why don't you go sit in the parlor, and I'll bring you somethin' to calm your nerves. I can only imagine what you have gone through." Kate nodded and got to her feet.

"I'll walk you," Boone said, offering her his uninjured arm. With an apologetic smile, she took it.

As they made their way from the dining room toward the parlor, Kate could feel her strength fading. She looked up, and to her surprise, the room was empty. Boone led them to a pair of armchairs by the window. After sitting, she watched the gossamer curtains shifting in the slight spring breeze. How had this happened? The anxious thrum of her heart forced her from her seated position, and she began to pace the room.

"Kate?" Boone's gentle voice made her jump. Whirling to face him, she collided with his strong chest. She had been so distracted by her own thoughts that she hadn't heard him walk up behind her.

Kate's heart started pounding furiously. Her thoughts went back to her shop where he'd held her briefly in his arms and protected her with his body. Her gaze drifted up to meet the stormy blue of his eyes, and her heart increased its already rapid tempo. Despite the unpleasantness of the day, she could stop thinking about her attraction to Boone.

He reached forward and took her hand in his. "Kate, I'm sorry I wasn't there sooner," he said, his voice deep and provocative.

"Oh?" Kate could hardly think straight.

"If I'd been there, Dixon wouldn't have tried anything in the first place." He had a pained expression in his eyes as his thumb rubbed the back of her hand.

Kate didn't want to think about that right now. Mr. Dixon wouldn't ruin her day any further, so she shook her head. "You came when I needed you most. And I shouldn't have lashed out at you as I did." She squeezed his hand in an effort to reassure him. "I am sorry."

He was silent for a moment, just looking at her, searching her eyes for something. *For what?* She didn't know. Her gaze momentarily flickered to his lips before going back to his eyes. In that moment, his narrow, hooded eyes widened and engulfed her in their dark depths, causing her breath to catch.

Tightening his hold on her hand, he pulled her toward him until they were only a few inches apart, the back of his other hand softly brushing her cheek. He cradled her face in his hand and pulled her face to his, their breath mingling.

"You'd better slap me, Kit, before I do something we might regret," he said.

Contemplating whether she should do as he asked, Kate decided that she wouldn't regret a kiss between them. She'd been longing for his affection for some time.

"I can't do that, Boone," she said, looking him in the eyes.

"Why not?"

Someone gasped behind them, and they leapt away from each other. Beth stood in the doorway, one hand still on the parlor door handle and the other covering her mouth, her eyes wide. "Oh, I didn't mean to interrupt." Boone chuckled, and Kate brought her hands to her cheeks, which she was sure were bright scarlet.

"Can't you give us a little privacy?" Boone asked, his face covered in a wide grin.

"Well, I'm not sure." Beth looked at Boone, her eyes narrowing slightly. "My ma said she saw the whole thing with Dixon and said that you might not be the kind of man we want in our town. And Kate," she faced Kate with a small pucker in her eyebrows, her lips turned down slightly, "Dixon said you've been leadin' him on and that you didn't mind his advances until Boone showed up today. Dixon's sayin' that you must have played both of them." Beth looked away. "And that people shouldn't buy from you anymore."

Kate felt her heart stop. If people listened to him, this would be the end of her shop. The end of her dream. What was she going to do?

Twelve

Five days had passed since the fight, and since that time, Boone had become even more alert and protective of Kate. She noticed that even though he continued to work outside, he would find any excuse to enter the shop if he heard the bell ring. Boone's presence kept Mr. Dixon at bay, but Kate felt a prick of irritation with Boone' insistence on protecting her.

"Boone, you need not walk with me. I am perfectly capable of getting to and from my shop alone," she said as they left the boarding house.

"I still have to finish your shelves. Besides, who knows when that brute will show up." Boone pulled the brim of his hat lower to block the sun while he peered around.

"He wouldn't dare after the beating you gave him."

Boone chuckled. "I appreciate your confidence but we'll still need to keep an eye out."

Though she was grateful to have Boone with her, she was keenly aware that he wasn't going to be there forever. And it seemed that everyone she crossed paths with in town wanted him to leave. As they walked down Main Street, she smiled at people as they passed, but no one smiled back.

They were walking by the mining supplies store when a tall, broad-shouldered man stepped through the swinging saloon doors just ahead of them. His hat was pulled low over his eyes. She could see the wisps of dark hair poke out from under the brim, and his long beard waved in the warm breeze. Something about his swaggering steps made her uneasy.

"Kate, is something wrong?" Boone asked, turning to look at her. She hadn't realized she had stopped walking.

"Did you see that stranger stepping out of the saloon just now?" She lowered her voice and tried not to call too much attention to herself as the stranger crossed the street toward the general store.

Kate tried to sound conversational, but the lump in her throat made it difficult to speak without her voice cracking. "Does he look like anyone to you?" she asked, still unsure of who the man could be.

Boone followed the man's movements, eyes narrowed.

The day had passed quickly, and Kate was surprised it was already time to close.

"Are you almost done?" Boone asked, putting the tools in the corner of her shop.

"Yes, after I put these supplies away." As she tidied the few materials for Beth's dress, Kate knew she would be done much sooner that she'd originally planned. The knowledge wasn't comforting though, and cleaning up after a day's work didn't take long anymore.

Kate sighed. The last five days had been slow, but today was the worst. People were talking about the fight, and most were siding with Mr. Dixon. For them, the brawl had been their first impression of Boone, and they didn't like what they saw. Kate supposed that all they had seen was an angry and violent soldier, though she knew that wasn't the truth.

When she had finished, Boone opened the door for her. "Let's go home," he said.

Something about the way Boone spoke delighted Kate. She wondered whether she was overtired and reading into things that weren't there, but her mind had already filled with dreams of a life with him. Since Boone had almost kissed her, she realized she had grown to care for him—far more than she had expected—and not just for his appearance. Any woman with eyes could appreciate Boone's attractiveness. But she had also seen his willingness to help people, his strength of character, and his tenacity, and he seemed to admire her independence. The more she learned about Boone, the more she wanted to know. Her heart contracted. *He is leaving after the wedding*, she reminded herself.

"Why are you looking at me like that?" Boone asked, his eyebrows quirked.

"Oh, no reason. I just forgot to do something." She whirled around and moved to her supplies, pretending to fiddle with something. She hoped the action had hid her blush.

"If you say so," he said, drawing out his reply. She heard the confusion in his voice. "But that reminds me,

I forgot something as well." He closed the door he had been holding for her and crossed to the back of her shop. "Lock up after I go out," he called as he left.

When Kate heard the back door shut, she released a small groan of embarrassment. She couldn't believe she had been caught staring at him again.

Knowing there was nothing else she needed to do, she locked the back door. She closed the curtains and put on her bonnet as she walked out the front door. Once the front door was locked, she stood on the boardwalk and looked around while she waited for Boone. The days were getting longer, and she enjoyed watching the sun's slow descent. Most families were gathered for dinner, and the town was quiet.

Suddenly, the hair on her neck stood on end, and chills coursed through her body. She had the unmistakable impression that someone was watching her. Her gaze swept around and landed on a hulking shadow in the alleyway across the street to her left. The glint of a ring caught her attention as the shadow faded farther into the darkness.

"All done." Boone's voice came from her left.

"Oh!" she gasped. Her heart thundered in her chest. "What?"

"You scared me," she said, wrapping her arms around herself.

"You knew I was still here," he said with a smirk.

"Yes, but...," she looked back at the alley, "I thought I saw someone watching me from over there." She nodded her head toward the ally.

Boone's expression became cold as he looked the same way. "I don't see anything now. Do you know who it was?"

She hesitated. "I didn't see their face, but I have an idea who was there."

"Dixon."

She nodded.

He took a step closer, his gaze intense. "I promise. No one's gonna hurt you while I'm here."

Kate wanted to smile at his words. She wondered whether he would consider staying if she asked him to.

"Does that mean you aren't going home?" She bit the inside of her cheek, worried that she might have sounded too hopeful.

"It's too soon to think about that right now."

She stepped away from him. "The wedding is less than four weeks away. You won't be here forever, but *he* will be." Fear coursed through her at the thought of what was going to happen when Boone went home to his family. Mr. Dixon would try again as soon as Boone rode away. She knew it, and the thought terrified her.

They made their way back to the boarding house in silence, both absorbed in their own thoughts and feelings.

"I, uh, think I left something else at your shop. Tell Charlotte I'll be back soon," Boone said. His eyes met Kate's for a brief moment, and she wanted to lean into him; she wanted to feel the warmth and security of his embrace again. She swallowed hard.

Kate nodded hesitantly. "Very well," she said, nodding slowly. Boone tipped the brim of his hat then turned away, walking briskly down the street. She stood on the porch and watched him until he disappeared around the corner.

Thirteen

Boone walked with purposeful strides down Main Street. He felt bad for lying to Kate about going back to her shop, but he needed to confront Dixon without worrying about her. Plus, she would have tried to talk him out of it.

He was almost at the street that led to Kate's shop and Dixon's house, when a man came stumbling out of the saloon. Even though it was getting darker, Boone could see the long beard and dirty clothes of the stranger from earlier that morning. The man didn't see him and started staggering in the same direction Boone was going. Not wanting to be discovered, Boone slowed his pace so the man wouldn't notice his presence.

The night sky was cloudy, providing the perfect cover for Boone as he followed the stranger straight to Dixon's house. Confused, Boone crouched low and moved in the shadows to avoid being seen as the man walked in without knocking.

Taking great care to be as silent as possible, Boone crept up to the open window of a small sitting room and knelt in the dirt, waiting for a sound. Boone raised himself slightly and peeked through the window, catching sight of Dixon and the stranger greeting each other in the hallway. The stranger was shorter than Dixon and more rotund, sporting a scraggly salt-and-pepper beard that hung nearly to his belly.

Boone shook his head. *How do these two know each other?*

They walked into the sitting room, and from the bits and pieces Boone heard, nothing seemed that suspicious. When they moved to the chairs by the window Boone was hiding under, he ducked quickly. Holding his breath, he ventured another peek and saw they had their back turned to him. Boone continued to watch them as he focused on their voices, trying to piece together their conversation.

"Ya left the saloon so early, Lez. Where'd ya go?" the shorter man asked, scratching at his beard. Boone wondered if he had fleas judging by how fiercely he was itching himself.

Dixon scoffed. "I hadta check on somethin'." He paused. "What're ya doin' here, Mathias?"

Mathias blew out an exasperated breath. "To be honest, I need some money."

"Run out again? I bailed ya out of yer last scrape, and that were only a year ago. I ain't helpin' again." Dixon shook his head.

"Why? You gotta have lots lying around still. And it's even in the Bible that ya oughta look after yer fellow men." The smaller man nodded once, as if his logic had won the argument.

Dixon let a string of profanities fly. "Weren't it last year ya came beggin' money off me to save yer life and pay yer debts?"

"Yeah."

"And I helped ya, but ya said ya wouldn't do it again?"

"Yeah."

Dixon sighed. "How much is it this time?"

Mathias didn't answer.

"Mathias, how much did ya lose?"

"I...I owe...I've got two weeks to get him 250 dollars, or he's gonna use me for target practice." As the words tumbled out of Mathias, he held his hands up as if anticipating Dixon's reaction.

Boone felt his jaw drop. *Mathias thinks Dixon can pay that off? How would he have gotten that much money?*

Dixon scoffed and shook his head. "Yer an idiot. I've got my own problems right now. While you've been burnin' up your money, I got the sheriff lookin' at me. And a stubborn woman worth her weight in—" Dixon stopped, cut short by his brother's words.

"Yeah, I heard you was in a fight and lost perty bad."

"Shut yer mouth! I only lost 'cause he fought dirty," Dixon said, pounding his fist on the table. "I'd like nothin' better than to rub that scum's face into the ground, but that'd bring bad attention. Last thing I need is my name goin' across the sheriff's desk again."

"Which name? Lez? Or Linus Warhol?" Mathias said.

Linus Warhol? Confusion flooded Boone's mind just as Dixon reached over and lightly shoved Mathias. "Don't call me that! At least not in town."

"But why, *Lez*?"

"It's short for Leslie, and nobody's gonna suspect a man named Leslie. Makes me seem softer." His voice turned mocking, and Mathias laughed.

"Speaking of town," Mathias said, "What are ya doing here, anyway? Yer spendin' money instead of makin' it. And you've got the sheriff suspicious. Not very productive for a man of your...line of work."

Dixon chuckled and put his legs on the table in front of them. "It may be frustratin', but it'll be worth it when it pays off. I ain't worried. This'll all blow over soon enough. Just gotta keep my head down."

"It's worked before," Mathias murmured.

"It sure has, brother. It sure has."

Their conversation drifted to trivial things, and Boone crept away from the house, concerned about what he'd heard. There was something strange going on with Dixon. *Or was his real name Linus Warhol? And what line of work?* Now that he thought about it, Boone didn't know what Dixon did in this town anyway. He didn't have a job. He just seemed to walk around, go to the saloon, and visit Kate.

Kate.

Maybe he'd discuss his thoughts with her. Boone valued her opinion more than anybody else's, but he wasn't sure it was wise at this point to burden her with all his suspicions.

He decided he'd wait and see what happened, not wanting to tell her in case she did something rash. Hopefully, his decision wouldn't cause her any more pain.

Fourteen

Unable to sleep any longer, Kate got out of bed and readied herself for the day. She wasn't sure whether the shadow in the alley last night had been Dixon, and the uncertainty had kept her up late. But she refused to let him ruin her life here, even if he was trying to ruin her business. Though her shop was struggling more than before, at least she had more time to work on organizing the show room and working on Beth's dress.

As she walked quietly into the empty kitchen to get herself some breakfast, she thought about the upcoming wedding. Each time she saw Beth's face light up when talking about her beloved, she found herself wanting to experience the same joy. At first, it was shocking to realize that Kate could still want love in her life after everything that had happened, but she was growing more accustomed to it and found herself thinking she would like to get married someday—as long as it was her choice.

Boone's face flashed through her mind as it often did these days. Her heart hammered when she recalled how he had almost kissed her. She felt her face flush at the thought, goose bumps racing over her skin. But anxiety quickly replaced her elation because while she secretly wanted him to try to kiss her again, he hadn't. It worried her further when he'd told her to stop him before he did something they would both regret. *Would he regret a kiss between them?*

She shook her head to dispel her thoughts and ate breakfast with an unusual fervor.

How did she know Boone wasn't just another version of Henry? They hadn't known each other that long, and Boone could just be on his best behavior right now. How could Kate know he wasn't just another scoundrel who would lead her on and break her heart?

She sighed. Despite her fears about Boone, she knew her attachment to him was growing daily. During their short time together, she had felt happier and more content than she had in all her time with her parents. Though this knowledge should have brought her joy and hope, she only felt a growing unease.

Boone had said from the start that he would be returning home after Beth and Jesse's wedding. And since he possibly regretted their almost kiss, Kate doubted there was anything she could do to entice him to stay.

The mounting confusion in Kate's mind suddenly turned to a fierce boil in her heart, and she leapt to her feet. "Enough!" she whispered forcefully to the empty room.

"Did I do something?" Boone's voice came from behind her.

She whirled around, hand flying to her chest to try and calm her rapidly beating heart.

Boone was leaning one shoulder against the door frame, his arms folded. With his whisker growth and disheveled hair, he looked better than ever, and Kate didn't realize her mouth had dropped open.

"Good...good morning, Mr. Carson," Kate said, struggling to get the words out.

"Morning, Miss Kit." He sent her a gorgeous smile, and Kate was proud of her ability to stay standing.

"Miss *Kate*," she said, emphasizing her name. "I hope I didn't wake you, but I decided to get an early start to the day." Her mouth was dry, and she didn't know what to do with her hands.

"You didn't, but I can walk you to your shop if you're ready to go."

Kate nodded but didn't move. She couldn't tear her eyes from him. If that table hadn't been between them, she might have been tempted to ask for that kiss.

"Miss Kit?" Boone said, sending her a quizzical look.

Kate realized that she had still been staring at him openmouthed. She closed her lips quickly.

"Right! I'll tidy these up and grab my things." She grabbed her dishes and turned to the water basin in embarrassment.

He chuckled. "I'll wait for you in the parlor," he said, and Kate heard his footsteps retreat.

Kate let out a heavy sigh. "How elegant," she muttered to herself.

A short while later, Kate and Boone exited the boarding house together and began the walk to Kate's shop. Boone offered his arm to her, and she took it, her senses tingling at his nearness.

"I have a confession," Boone said in a hushed tone.

Kate was intrigued. "And what might that be?"

"I've noticed that you don't correct me anymore when I don't call you Miss Morrison. Don't get me wrong. I'm glad, and I commend you on your progress." His voice held a hint of teasing, but the combination of his words and his intonation still sent a thrill through her.

Quickly pulling herself together, she nodded. "I suppose I grew tired of dealing with your stubbornness on that matter. I think it would be wise for me to save my energy for more pressing matters in the future. Although, I haven't given up on getting you to call me Miss Kate." She tried to look serious, but a smile broke through anyway.

Boone laughed, and the sound warmed her heart.

They walked in comfortable silence for a few minutes, but her fears about his plans after the wedding were fresh on her mind. Truthfully, she also yearned to hear his voice, no matter what they talked about.

"I imagine you miss your home and family terribly, Mr. Carson. How soon after the wedding do you think you'll leave to see them?" Surprised by her own forwardness, Kate found that she was holding her breath as she waited for his reply.

Boone seemed pensive for a moment. "I do miss my family, but I confess, Brexton is starting to feel more and more like home. And I don't miss ranch work. I love my home because of the people, not because of the house."

Out of the corner of her eye, Kate saw Boone turn his head to her. With some effort, she kept her own gaze fixed ahead. She didn't know whether she could keep herself composed if she looked back at him.

He continued while still looking at her. "I originally thought I'd leave a day or two after the wedding, which would give me time to prepare my things and say goodbye to everyone."

Kate's stomach lurched. That meant she only had four weeks left with Boone before he rode away. She risked a glance at him and found him watching her intently. She forced a smile to her face. "I'm sure your family cannot wait for you to return."

Boone shrugged. "They've said as much in their letters," he said. "But other than my injury, I've enjoyed my stay in Brexton. It's beautiful land, and the weather is warmer than it is at home. The people are friendly—well, they were before my business with Dixon. But it's just so wonderful. I don't really feel like leaving."

It might not be as beautiful when you leave, Kate thought grimly.

But Boone continued. "And there are certain people here that make it more appealing." Kate's hope soared.

"Take Jesse, for instance. I like having a friend I can trust and rely on. I never really had that growing up. Sure, I had my brother, but there's a different kind of trust between Jesse and me. We lived and fought for each other."

Kate's hope deflated.

Boone kept going. "And Charlotte is great. I would stay just for her cooking. I might even ask for her to adopt me." He laughed. "There are many fine people here, and I've a mind to stay longer." He smiled at her warmly.

Kate forced another smile but had a hard time feeling happy for him. She had hoped he would list her as one of Brexton's finer qualities—but he hadn't. He might stay

"That might be true, but I spent most of my money on this place. But I got a plan to get it all back and then some, brother."

Boone's eyes widened in surprise. *Brother?*

"What plan?" Mathias asked, leaning closer. "Ya know I could help ya." Boone could practically hear the greed in the man's voice.

"Mathias, if yer so desperate for money, go sell the stuff Mama left ya after she passed. I won't hold it against ya." Dixon's voice softened.

Mathias ducked his head. Boone watched his hands come up and rub his face. Dixon groaned. "Don't tell me ya already did?"

Mathias shrugged. "I sold everything about a week after I got 'em. And don't call me Mathias anymore."

Why doesn't he want to be called by his name?

Dixon put his face in his hands and shook his head, groaning. "Yer such an idiot."

"I ain't no idiot," Mathias said, leaping to his feet and knocking over the chair he had been sitting on.

"Yeah, ya are, so sit down and shut up about it." The chair scraped the floor as Mathias picked it up and then sat down, grumbling.

"I just need some money, and I know ya still got some. I don't need much, just enough for..." Mathias trailed off then.

"Enough for what?"

"Just...stuff."

"What kinda stuff ya talkin' 'bout? Gamblin' stuff?"

Mathias mumbled, "Yeah."

longer, but eventually, he would go back home. If he ever returned, she knew it wouldn't be because of her, no matter how much she wanted it to be so.

Kate decided that keeping her feelings hidden was best at this point. There was no sense in falling for another potential Henry.

As they walked, Boone's arm brushed against hers. She glanced at him and found a mischievous smile had pulled at the corner of his mouth.

A silence lulled between them as they turned onto her street, but this time, Kate felt uncomfortable. As they neared her shop, her discomfort grew, and she realized it wasn't because of Boone or his plans to leave. She had the same feeling that had crept upon her last night. Turning her head, she looked across the street to see if her instinct was true.

Standing directly across from her shop, glaring hatefully at her and Boone, was Mr. Dixon.

Boone felt Kate stiffen just before she stopped walking. Her abrupt stop detached her arm from his, and Boone turned his head in the direction she was looking. Mr. Dixon stood across the street, leaning on a post. The large man's mouth curled into a twisted smile when he saw Kate's reaction to him.

Boone heard her breath quicken, and he could see her hands were trembling, although she tried to hide them behind her straightening back.

Anger at what Dixon was putting Kate through flared in Boone, and he stepped toward Kate, putting his arm around her shoulders and pulling her closer to him. Dixon stood up straight, his smile contorting into a nasty sneer. Boone felt Kate wrap her arms around herself. He hated that Dixon made her feel this way.

"Let's get you into the shop," Boone whispered into her ear, and she shivered but nodded.

Boone turned back and glared at Dixon, who just spat in the dirt and walked farther down the street.

Still holding Kate's shaking shoulders, he guided her to the door of her shop. Boone dropped his hands from her as she unlocked the door and hurried inside. He looked down the street for Dixon, but the man was out of sight. Sighing, Boone entered the shop.

Dixon was getting bolder in his advances, and Boone didn't know what to do. He didn't know what this man was capable of, and he didn't want to find out. However, Boone knew that whatever Dixon wanted was surely going to hurt Kate. But how was Boone going to protect her without knowing what Dixon was planning? Boone's frustration with the situation grew, but he supposed that his only option was to stay with Kate and watch until Dixon made his move.

Boone watched as Kate bustled around, readying the shop for the day's work. He'd soon have to head back to help Jesse work on the house he'd share with Beth, but Boone couldn't move.

Even though Boone and Kate's first meeting was a dramatic one, everything he'd learned about her since then made him admire her all the more. She'd sacrificed time with her new business to help him—a grumpy and rude stranger—to heal from a life-threatening wound. Not many people were that compassionate and selfless.

Boone thought about her determination and bravery. Though he didn't know her whole story, he knew she had a tremendous amount of courage and tenacity to come to Brexton and begin building a life on her own. He felt like a coward for not telling her about his arrangement to this Miss Kingston whom he had never met, especially after almost kissing Kate. But he lacked the bravery; it had been easier to face an army of Rebs than consider telling Kate his secret.

She had quickly become one of the most interesting people he'd ever met, and he took great pride in keeping her safe from Dixon. In spite of all the things that she'd done for him, Boone doubted that she realized he'd found a sense of purpose again because of her. He had been a broken man when he'd fallen at her feet. Slowly and unknowingly, however, Kate had built him up and stripped away the ugly bruises on his heart that he had received from the war. If only she knew how much he was in her debt.

A realization hit Boone hard, and it felt like he suddenly had fresh eyes. He couldn't believe he had been so blind to this woman. The way she floated around the room humming softly to herself. The quiet confidence she always seemed to have—even when her hand shook or tears rolled unwanted down her soft pink cheeks.

With an incredulous smile, Boone accepted the fact that he could never marry anyone other than Kate Morrison. She was the kindest, most hardworking, wonderful, beautiful woman he'd ever met. Inside and out. And he'd fallen in love with her. With that knowledge, he was more determined than ever to keep her safe.

"Kit?" he said, breaking the silence.

"Hmm?" She didn't look up from the bolts of fabric she was taking down from the newly finished shelf. "It's Miss Kate," she said, her lips pressing together with a slight upturn at the corners.

He paused for a moment, smiling at her tease, and continued. "I've got to head back to help Jesse, but before I go...do you feel safe?"

She stopped what she was doing and turned to face him.

Wrinkling her nose, she said, "Yes...no...well, sometimes." She dropped her head before looking at him.

Boone walked over and took her hands in his, but she looked down. Gently, he put his finger under her chin and tipped her face up. His heart did a somersault when she looked at him with her beautiful brown eyes. He swallowed the lump in his throat. "Sometimes?"

She sighed in defeat. "Oh, Boone. I've felt so uneasy since I met Mr. Dixon, especially when I'm somewhere he can talk to me alone. He scares me even though I say I can take care of myself." She bit her lip, and Boone could tell this was difficult for her to admit. He nodded, urging her to continue even though his heart now beat furiously as soon as she'd used his first name instead of his last. She didn't seem to realize it and kept going.

"But that changed when...when you arrived. Whenever you're around, I feel safer than I've ever felt. But soon, you're going to leave Brexton. I fear what will happen once you do." She looked out the window then, her face uneasy.

Boone sighed. He stroked the back of her hands with his thumbs. She might not admit it, but he knew her stubborn strength was waning.

She turned back to Boone, and her words flowed out quickly. "But it's not fair of me to ask you to stay and keep me safe. You can't be here all the time, but sometimes I want to be selfish and ask you to please stay here and help me. Talk to me, build my shelves, laugh with me, hold me, and—" Kate gasped, one hand flew to her mouth, and she tried to step away, but Boone held fast to her other hand. The pink in her cheeks transformed to her usual scarlet, and she turned her entire body to hide her face. Boone's heart hammered with the emotions her confession stirred in him. He could tell she enjoyed his company, but he had no idea her feelings for him might be stronger. Were they similar at all to what he felt for her?

"Kit?"

She only shook her head, still trying to pull away from him.

He stepped closer. "Kate."

Kate's body pulsed with hot waves of embarrassment. *Why did I say that to him?* She couldn't look at him and see the rejection in his eyes. But at the sound of her name—not her nickname—she paused. He had said it so tenderly, so intimately. She breathed in all the courage she could muster and turned back to him.

The adoration in his eyes was so starkly apparent that Kate's breath sucked in sharply, and a smile began growing on her face. He held her hand with his own, and with the other he caressed the back of her arm. Shivers of excitement replaced her embarrassment.

"I would very much like to help you. With *everything* you just mentioned," Boone said. He was close enough that she could feel the breath of his words.

"Really?" Her hand slipped from covering her mouth. Was she dreaming?

Boone's lips widened into a magnificent smile. "I've been wanting to hold—I mean help—you for some time now," he said, chuckling.

"Really?" Why wouldn't her brain let her say something else?

"Really." He lifted his hand to her face and brushed the hair away. Goosebumps scattered everywhere as he placed his hand on her cheek.

His gaze became more intense, and Kate forgot to breathe. His thumb lightly passed over her bottom lip as his head descended toward hers. The first touch of their lips was barely discernible, but it shook Kate to her core.

The second was more firmly applied, and the third even more so. By the fourth kiss, Kate wasn't sure how she stayed standing. She was convinced her legs would crumple beneath her.

I could kiss him forever, she thought blissfully. *In fact, I could love him forever.* The thought shocked her, and she broke the kiss and backed out of Boone's arms.

She loved Boone. She loved Boone, and he was going to leave. Her heart strained with simultaneous elation and heartbreak.

"Is something wrong?" Boone asked.

If only you knew. Kate shook her head. "I thought I heard a customer come in. But I guess not." It was a lie, but she thought it was necessary.

Boone nodded slowly then stepped forward, closing the gap between them. He pulled Kate to him and slipped his arms around her waist, embracing her. Her own arms wrapped around his neck, and she clung to him. The thought of him leaving was painful, but his embrace comforted her anyway.

He pulled his head back and placed it on her forehead, still holding her. "I don't want to, but I need to go help Jesse." He released her from his arms. "But I'll be back this afternoon to escort you home." His mouth curled into a mischievous smile, and he wiggled his eyebrows at her.

Kate laughed at his playfulness.

Boone turned to leave, but when he reached the door, he stopped. "I'm glad you feel safe with me, Kate." Then he left, the bell tinkling in his wake.

"No, Boone." Kate whispered to the empty room. "You are my greatest risk."

Kate spent most of the morning working on three different projects. Mrs. Melbourne's daughter needed a formal dress, but Mrs. Melbourne had been hesitant to give Kate her business at first. Though Kate had finished the dress the day before, there were still a few finishing touches to work on, and she wanted the dress to be perfect so that Mrs. Melbourne wouldn't regret her decision.

As she added the last details, Kate heard the shop's bell jingle.

She put on a friendly smile in spite of the distress she was feeling over her situation with Boone. "Hello, how can I...," but her words caught in her throat.

Mr. Dixon walked forward and stopped directly in front of her. She raised her chin up and stood tall, but she was still dwarfed by him. Her mind silently called out for Boone.

"What do you want?" she asked, folding her arms to stop them from trembling.

"What do I want?" he asked, rocking on his heels, his putrid breath wafting around her. "I want you."

Kate's eyes widened.

Mr. Dixon kept going. "I've been wanting ya for a long time now." He started pacing. "I started comin' by and bein' nice. I even helped ya with yer business. Did ya know I pulled those buttons off just before I came to the shop?"

Kate had known, but she had still needed the money.

"But you...," he said, pointing his finger in her face, "You played coy with me and led me on."

Kate's mouth dropped open in astonishment. "I did no such thing!"

"Yes, ya did. But as soon as a nearly dead soldier rides into town, ya looked down yer nose at me and went to him."

He was clearly agitated, and his voice was rising. *Is he going to hurt me?* Kate shuddered.

Smiling lewdly, he leaned closer as she stepped back. "I tried to give ya a taste of the good time we could have together." He reached for her, and his ring flashed bright as his hand came closer.

Kate's stomach rolled, and she dashed behind the counter.

"I tried, but that dirty soldier got in the way. Twice," he said, holding up two large fingers.

"You need to leave, Mr. Dixon," Kate said, barely keeping her voice under control. Her emotions were already heightened, and Mr. Dixon was going to make her anger explode.

"I know if he wasn't around, ya wouldn't push me away so much. Just come with me. We can even stop at the preacher's house first if ya wanna. It's neither here nor there to me. Just give me one day, and I'll prove to ya how that dirty soldier ain't worth nothin'." He licked his lips and looked at her ravenously. "Waddya say, Kate? Are ya ready to be mine?"

That was it. The last straw. Kate's anger and fears because of Lez Dixon's harassment burst within her, and she slammed her hands on the counter.

"What do I say? You listen to me, you disgusting beast!"

Mr. Dixon's eyes widened in shock, and he even took a step back.

Kate pointed a finger at him. "Your attentions to me—if you can call them that—have been the most vile, abhorrent, and repulsive experiences I've ever had in my life." Thoughts of her mother and Henry filled her mind, and she directed her anger at them to her tirade against Mr. Dixon.

"Never once have I given you a reason to pursue me, and the only reason I let you come into my shop was for business. Obviously, that was all a ruse on your part, so you are now officially banned from coming in here ever again, business or not."

Mr. Dixon's face grew ugly with anger, but Kate wasn't done. Her dam had broken, and there was no stopping it.

"Furthermore, Boone Carson is more of a man than you ever will be. I would choose him over you every single day of my life."

Kate had found her strength, but Mr. Dixon's chest rose and fell with what looked like barely controlled fury.

"In fact, even if he wasn't here, I still wouldn't choose you. I would rather be a spinster. I respect myself too much to be further degraded by you." She pointed to the door. "Mr. Dixon, you leave my shop at once, and never, ever come back!"

Silence fell between them, and Kate's ears thudded with her own heartbeat, but she'd never felt more liberated. Even her tumultuous thoughts about her mother and Henry had seemed to fade.

The bell rang once more, and Mrs. Melbourne entered the shop, a skeptical look on her face.

"Mrs. Melbourne," Kate said, hoping her voice sounded cheerful. "Your daughter's dress is there on the dress form. I hope you're pleased with it."

Kate glanced at Mr. Dixon as Mrs. Melbourne walked over to the dress. An eel-like smile crossed his face, and dread filled Kate's chest.

"I'd be careful doin' business with Miss Kate," he said to Mrs. Melbourne. "She just tried to charge me double her original quote. Mighty unprofessional if you ask me."

Kate stared at him openmouthed as he sauntered to the door.

"That's disgraceful Miss Morrison," Mrs. Melbourne said, flinging the fabric out of her hands. "I think I'll take Harriet to Mrs. Brown's shop and buy a ready-made dress instead. Good day."

Mr. Dixon opened the door for the woman and gave her a polite goodbye. He looked back at Kate. "I wonder what yer gonna do when ya lose all yer business and yer shop? I sure hope you have a family to run back to. It ain't good for a girl perty as you to be alone." He threw her a triumphant grin and left the shop.

Shocked, Kate fell back into her chair and stared at the door. She watched as several young ladies and their mothers walked by, looked in the shop's windows, then turned their noses up once they caught sight of Kate inside. If Mr. Dixon had the ability to keep an entire town from going to her shop, what else was he capable of? More importantly, she didn't know whether she'd finally driven him off or whether his desire for her had only grown. That thought terrified her most.

Fifteen

Kate was working on Beth's wedding dress when Boone returned to the shop at lunchtime. "I...I got the last of the supplies to finish that...that shelf in the back," he said. "Are you...are you ready for lunch?" He seemed a little jumpy and hesitant, making Kate's stomach start churning again, but for different reasons than earlier.

"I am," she said, searching his face for any hint of what was on his mind. "Let me lock up first, then I'll join you." But she couldn't move. Did he regret their kiss? Had Mr. Dixon spoken to him?

They stood in an awkward silence for a few moments until Kate couldn't stand it any longer. "Is something wrong? Did something happen?"

Boone was looking everywhere in the room except at her. He'd open his mouth to say something then close it again a moment later. Kate's heart sank lower and lower. Whatever it was, it couldn't be pleasant.

"Just tell me what's going on, Boone," Kate said.

Finally, he looked at her, and she could see the conflict in the turbulent blue of his eyes. He let out a defeated sigh. "I need to talk to you about something."

Dread began to fill her. "About what?"

"I...I don't..." He wouldn't meet her eyes.

"Just tell me," Kate whispered.

He sighed and extended his hand to her. She took it and allowed him to pull her into a loose embrace.

Boone leaned back and rubbed his eyes with one hand. He sighed before looking at her. "I...there's a...it started when I wrote my mama..."

Kate had never heard him stumble over his words. He seemed so nervous and uncertain.

"Boone," she said softly, "just tell me."

Staring blankly at her, Boone stroked her face absently with his finger, sending warm chills down her spine.

Boone closed his eyes. "Kate, technically, I'm engaged."

Kate froze and, for the next few minutes, everything was hazy. She felt like the ground had just dropped out from under her feet. It was only a few hours ago that Kate had admitted to herself that she loved Boone. And now, he was suddenly promised to another. Anger, pain, and betrayal surged through her like a fiery wave.

Slowly, she became aware of Boone holding her hands and then her face. Kate felt as though she were overheating. She needed to be as far away from him as possible.

Not again! she thought in anguish.

Boone was speaking to her, but her mind could not comprehend what he was trying to say. She shook her head slightly and moved away from him—but he gripped her arms gently and pulled her back. The pounding ache in her head and heart was still drowning out any other sounds.

"...that's what I told her. Kate, please. You have to believe me." He sounded desperate. She hadn't heard everything Boone had said, but she didn't need to.

He was just another Henry.

"Please say you believe me, Kate," he whispered, leaning his forehead on hers.

His head against hers brought Kate back to reality with a thundering jolt. Shaking her head and ripping herself from Boone's grasp, she backed away. "You and Dixon and Henry are all the same!" She pointed a threatening finger at Boone. "I am not a toy for your amusement, or someone to occupy you until someone you really want comes along!"

"Kate, no. You don't understand." Boone tried to reach for her again, but she sidestepped his outstretched arms.

"I understand plenty. You never cared for me. You're just like them."

Boone shook his head. "No! That ain't it at all. Didn't you hear what I said?" He took another step closer but stopped when Kate sent him a withering look.

"You need to leave. Now!" Kate said, each word clipped. She stormed to the door and threw it open.

"Kate, please listen to..."

"You are no longer welcome in my shop Mr. Carson." She couldn't believe she'd had to ban two men in one morning.

Boone stood there; his mouth was agape, and he just stared at her before he strode out the door.

Once Kate was sure he wasn't coming back, she locked both entrances and closed the curtains. Mr. Dixon had made sure she wouldn't have any customers anymore, so what was the point of staying open?

The weight of what had happened finally crushed her heart, and she sank to the ground, sobbing. How could she have been so stupid to fall for another Henry?

Kate wasn't sure how long she cried for. She sat on the ground long after the tears had stopped flowing. The only sound was her own shaky breath as she watched the sun's rays move across her shop.

She startled when she heard a knocking at the door. She leapt to her feet and tried to freshen up her face. She prayed it wasn't Boone or Mr. Dixon and hoped it was a client. Kate unlocked the door and threw open the curtains. One customer was better than none.

But she should've ignored the knock.

Mr. Dixon turned the door handle and pushed his way into the shop. Kate was no match for his strength and was shoved away from the door.

"It's a shame that yer shop is so empty right now," he said, feigned concern pasted on his face.

"Yes, I am sure you must be so worried," Kate said, her tone biting.

"I thought I saw yer beloved Boone stormin' through town earlier. I've come back to ask if you'd like to reconsider my offer. I can make all yer troubles go away," he said, holding out his hand.

Kate scoffed incredulously and shook her head. "You must be the biggest idiot in this country. I have already said I will never be with you, and nothing has or ever will change my mind. Now leave!" She pointed to the door.

Mr. Dixon's rage was clearly threatening to explode, but an unfamiliar man's voice called his name, and he looked out the door briefly.

"Yer gonna regret this," he said before leaving the shop and slamming the door behind him.

Kate shook her head, turning around and leaning against the door. "No, you are not what I regret the most today."

Boone was still agitated. He'd been planning what he would say to Kate the whole walk over. When he tried to explain, though, Kate had reacted far worse than he'd imagined she would. He'd just received his mama's letter with answers to his questions. As soon as he read it, he knew he needed to share his situation with Kate. *Where had it all gone so horribly wrong?*

In one moment, he felt guilty for not being honest with her sooner. But in the next, his anger would flare. How dare she assume he'd get close to a woman if he had a sweetheart waiting at home? Did Kate really think so little of him?

Boone waited at the boarding house for her to come home for lunch, but she never did. Charlotte and Jesse had tried to talk to him, but his agitated mind could not support a conversation with them. The only person he wanted to talk to wanted nothing to do with him.

After a few hours of slamming things around outside, he knew what he had to do. Kate needed to know that she had misunderstood him. Maybe she hadn't even heard him in the first place. He'd explain what had happened to him during the war and how he now no longer wanted the arranged marriage he'd asked for. All he wanted was her. This plan calmed him down, so he finally sat in the parlor to wait for her to come home.

"She's still not back?" Charlotte asked, bringing Boone something to eat. The sun had set, and the boarding house was dark, save for a few oil lamps.

Boone shook his head. "No, but I plan to wait till she is, and then I'll talk to her. This is all just a big misunderstanding."

Charlotte nodded thoughtfully and put the food on the small table beside him. "I hope she listens to ya, Boone. You've truly brought out the best in each other. She's more open and happier, and ya ain't so angry at the world anymore. Anyone who knows either of ya knows that you've become stronger together."

Just then, they heard the outside door to the kitchen open. Boone leapt to his feet, quickly walking toward the sound. Charlotte stopped him and whispered, "Let me get her some food first. People don't listen well on an empty stomach."

Exerting every ounce of patience he had, Boone forced himself to sit back in the armchair and wait. He heard the women talking briefly but couldn't make out what they were saying or what Kate's mood was. Trying to get comfortable, he shifted around in his seat before giving up and leaning forward with his elbows on his knees and his hands supporting his chin. He stared intently at the door she would eventually come through to go up the stairs. Dishes clinked, and soft footfalls came in his direction.

Boone stood, but it was Charlotte who came through the door.

"She doesn't want to see you," she whispered, putting her finger to her lips.

"That's because she's thinking something that ain't true," he said, unwilling to listen to Charlotte's hushing. "I've gotta talk to Kate and make this right."

Charlotte put her hands on her hips and gave Boone a stern look. "Well then, go ahead. If you're so bound and determined right now to fix whatever happened between you two, then be my guest."

Boone took a step but stopped when Charlotte put a hand up. "But I warn ya, if you take your stubborn hide in there and try to patch this up now, you will make a bigger mess, and you will certainly lose her. For good."

Charlotte's words made Boone pause and take a step back. "How do ya know that?"

Charlotte sighed. "She didn't say anythin' to me, but whatever happened broke her heart. That much I can tell."

"Then what should I do, Miss Charlotte?" he pleaded. "She thinks I've got a fiancée waiting for me back home. She's got it in her head that I'm being unfaithful."

"That's a pretty big misunderstanding. What did you say to put that idea in her head?"

"Oh. Well, I told her that I...I was technically en-gaged—"

"What?" Charlotte hissed, her eyes flying wide open.

Boone shook his hands. "No. I asked my parents to arrange a marriage for me before the war ended. You saw me when I was healing. I had nothing to offer a woman, and I didn't want to go through the process of finding one. I just wanted a content life. I didn't think I deserved anything else. Not until I met Kate."

Charlotte shook her head. "You do beat all, boy. And I might beat you anyway if you survive this. But you need to give her tonight to settle, or this conversation won't go the way you hope. Not tonight."

"But I can't just do nothing!"

"Yes, you can. If you care for her at all, you can and you will," Charlotte said.

Boone hung his head in defeat and nodded solemnly.

"Maybe you should write down what you want to say to her," Charlotte said, giving his shoulder a motherly pat.

His head perked up at that. "I think I will. Good night, Miss Charlotte. And thank you," Boone said, turning around and walking to his room.

He sat down and wrote a letter, signing his name with purpose. But when he heard Kate's footsteps go past his door toward the stairs, his self-control fled, and he ran out of his room with the letter in his hand.

"Kate, please," he said.

Her foot was already on the first step, but slowly she turned around to look at him. Boone was racked with guilt when he saw that Kate's eyes were red and puffy. It crushed his heart to know that she was crying because of him.

As he walked closer, her eyes filled with anger. He was a little annoyed that the misunderstanding had pushed her to be so angry at him, but he forced his feelings aside. She had to know what he wrote in his letter.

Boone looked down. "Kate, I—"

"Miss Morrison."

His head snapped up. "Pardon?"

"You may call me Miss Morrison, Mr. Carson." She folded her arms and glared at him.

Boone swallowed the retort itching to escape his lips. Instead, he extended the letter. "Miss Morrison, if you'd be so kind as to read this letter, I think you'll find it clears up our misunderstanding."

She sneered at his outstretched hand. "Forgive me if I don't seem eager to accept it, Mr. Carson. I refuse to be a part of this game you're playing."

"Dang it all, woman!" He was shouting then, despite the late hour. "I'm trying to fix this!"

Kate shook her head and clicked her tongue. "Tsk, tsk. I wonder if your future bride knows about your temper."

"Oh, you have no idea," he said under his breath, locking his eyes on her. After all, she was the only bride he wanted. Kate's gaze shifted, and a flash of confusion crossed her face for a moment. He watched her shake her head then resume glaring at him.

Boone took a deep breath and held the letter closer to her. "Please? Will you just read it?"

Kate's face didn't change, but she took the letter and walked to the parlor. Boone was relieved that she had accepted it. He followed her in, feeling hopeful that they would resolve this debacle quickly. As she sat down in the same armchair that he had been waiting for her in, he wondered whether he should leave and let her read the letter alone.

But Boone didn't have the chance to decide.

In the next moment, Kate ripped the letter into pieces and plunged them into the glass of water Charlotte had brought out for Boone earlier that night.

"What are you doing?" he shouted, lunging forward. Kate stood and walked away from Boone and toward the stairs. He tried to fish the unread remnants of the letter from the water but quickly gave up. "I was going to send that to my mama after you read it," he said, glaring at her.

"It seems that neither of us will be able to read it now," Kate said, walking upstairs. "Have a pleasant night, Mr. Carson."

Groaning in frustration, Boone shook his head and wondered why he was fighting so hard to keep such a stubborn woman in his life. *Because I love her. That's why*, he thought.

Kate raced up the stairs. Heart pounding, she slammed the door shut and leaned up against it. She knew she didn't have the strength to see him again. Fresh tears began to rush down her face. She wiped at them angrily, but they only flowed more profusely.

Sobbing harder, Kate fell into her bed, hugging a pillow close to her chest. *How could he do this to me? And to her?*

Boone had tricked her and led her on, knowing full well that he had never actually been available. Her sobs came in great gasps, and her body shook with anguish. And yet, despite everything that she now knew, she still loved him. That knowledge was surely going to shatter her heart.

She sat upright in bed. *I can't be in the same room as him. I won't survive.* The only possible solution was to spend every moment she could in her shop—regardless of whether she had any customers left. She could spend time with Charlotte and Beth again after Boone left Brexton. It was the only solution she could think of, so it would have to do.

Lying back down, Kate curled herself into a ball. Boone would leave soon, and Kate would finally be able to find some peace. But, as much as she needed him to go, thinking of Boone building a life with another woman and leaving Kate at the mercy of Mr. Dixon made her ache until she started sobbing harder. After some time, sleep eventually dragged her into its dark embrace.

Sixteen

The tentative knock on the door brought Kate to full consciousness.

"Hey, stranger." Beth pushed the door open a crack. "Are you well?"

"No, but I will be." Kate sighed as she pushed herself into a sitting position. Her eyes were swollen, and her body was stiff from lack of sleep. "Why are you here so early? Don't you need to help your mama?"

"Jesse told me you had a fallin' out with Boone. Between all that time you've been spending together, Charlotte's inklings, and that almost kiss I walked in on..., I thought you two were on the way to gettin' serious." Beth handed Kate some freshly baked bread, and Kate accepted it gratefully.

"Thank you," Kate said as she took a bite.

"Do you wanna talk about it?"

Kate paused her chewing. "No, not until he leaves."

Beth nodded her head solemnly.

Kate guessed the cause of Beth's distress. "Don't worry. Your beautiful day will not be ruined because of Mr. Carson and me. We care about you and Jesse too much to let our issues cloud your happiness."

"Oh, Kate. I hope you don't think of me as that shallow. I want my weddin' to be beautiful, but I also want my friends to be happy."

"Well, you don't need to worry. There won't be any guest more joyful than me," Kate said with a grin.

Beth wrapped her arms around Kate. After a moment, Beth asked, "When will you talk to Boone?"

Kate sighed and shook her head. "I won't. He is engaged to someone else." Kate rubbed her face with her hands. "I cannot believe I fell for another Henry," she said in a whisper.

"Who's Henry?" Beth asked quietly.

"He is..." Kate sighed. "He is a man I used to know. I promise I will tell you the story one day, but it's too hard right now." She put a hand on Beth's shoulder. "But I will tell you that Mr. Carson and Henry have the nature of scoundrels and cads, and I was tricked by them both. I am glad to be rid of them."

Beth was quiet for a moment. "I know you're hurtin' right now, but I gotta be honest. I don't think you're seein' the whole picture."

Kate felt some annoyance at Beth's words but tried to force it down. "What makes you say that?"

Beth shrugged. "There's just a few things that people have noticed."

"Such as?"

"Well, people talk to me. The fight between Boone and Mr. Dixon made people pay more attention. Some see Boone as a protector of virtue, but now others believe what Dixon said about your business. The town's opinion is split on whether to side with Boone or Dixon. I've told them Boone wasn't at fault. I know people have been listenin' to what I told them 'cause their attitudes are startin' to change. I've even talked to a few people who've seen you two walkin' down the street together and lookin' happy. Many people, myself included, have made predictions that you and Boone might...," Beth looked sheepish, "might get hitched someday."

Kate felt heat rise to her cheeks. "Maybe that is what could have been, but I will never let that happen now that I know the truth."

"I still don't think Boone would be so blatantly unfaithful," Beth said, her voice kind but firm. "Jesse never even knew about Boone having a beau at home, and they spent so much time together. If Jesse had known, he wouldn't have let Boone spend so much time alone with you."

Kate pondered what Beth had said. "Maybe so, but he told me himself he was engaged."

"Are you sure that's the whole story? Talk to him. Learn the whole situation, and then make a decision."

"I will think about it. Thank you for the bread and the encouragement," Kate said, opening the door, "but I have to get to the shop now." Beth sighed but said goodbye and then left.

Once Kate finished dressing, she hurried down the stairs as quickly and quietly as she could. But her efforts were thwarted when she saw Boone sitting in the parlor, evidently waiting to escort her to the shop.

Boone jumped to his feet and grabbed his hat. "Morning, Ki—I mean, Miss Morrison."

Kate had thought about taking Beth's advice, but seeing him there brought all of her anger back to the surface.

"I won't be needing your help anymore, Mr. Carson. Stay away from me," Kate said, brushing past him. She moved across the parlor quickly and opened the door to leave.

"Kate, wait for—"

But she slammed the door before he could finish. Kate decided she would need to sneak out earlier from now on if she was going to avoid him.

The morning sun had already begun to warm the world as Kate hurried to her shop. It was still early, and she only saw a few people on Main Street. A few smiled or nodded, and the rest avoided her, just like Beth had said. Mr. Dixon's lies hadn't helped her already difficult circumstances. "Incorrigible man," she said, muttering under her breath.

At the thought of Mr. Dixon, Kate realized that this was the first time in a while that she'd walked to work without Boone's company. For a moment, she missed the peace of mind he'd provided.

When she turned onto her shop's street, the hair on the back of her neck rose, and she instinctively looked around for Mr. Dixon but didn't see anyone. She quickened her pace. The sound of footsteps across the street startled her, and she broke into a run. At her shop, she fumbled with the key before finally unlocking the door and rushing inside. Whirling around, she hastily banged the door shut and relocked it.

Her heart was thudding in her chest as she peeked through the curtains to see whether Dixon had followed her. But all she could see was the shape of someone disappearing around the corner onto the main street.

I wish Boone were here. The thought came to her before she could stop it. "No, I don't," she said to the fabric on the shelves—the shelves Boone had made for her. She groaned in frustration.

She didn't unlock her shop for another hour, hoping to avoid an encounter with Boone or Mr. Dixon.

As the day wore on, Kate's frustration and anger grew. How dare they! How dare Boone play with her feelings, making her fall in love with him when he had no intentions to stay with her. How dare Mr. Dixon ruin her prospects of running a successful business all because she had rejected his foul advances. She was getting more and more infuriated, and her thoughts moved to her past. How dare her parents try to control her life through any and every means possible? How dare Henry pretend to have feelings for her so that he could satisfy his love of money? She thought she had loved Henry, but when he'd betrayed her, he had only cracked her heart. Boone had ripped it to pieces.

But most of all, how dare she—Kate Morrison—let all these people trample over her dreams.

Lunch time came and went, but Kate had lost her appetite. She was working on a section of embroidery detail for Beth's wedding dress when the bell above the door announced someone's arrival.

She glanced up, hoping to see a customer, but she only saw an irate Boone.

"Go away, Mr. Carson," she warned, and she stood up.

"Kit, will you please listen to me?" Boone asked.

"No, and do not call me that!" She glared at him. "Get out." She picked up the pin cushion from the table and threw it at his head. It missed and bounced harmlessly to the floor, but the look on his face showed his anger intensifying. *He* was angry? *The nerve.*

"Have it your way then." He stepped out of the doorway and left.

Tears threatened to fall down her cheeks, but she forced them back. Kate watched him stomp toward Main Street, his limp still noticeable, until he was around the corner and out of her sight. She rubbed her weary eyes and sighed before getting back to work.

And what dismal work it was. Since yesterday's encounter with Mr. Dixon, no one had come into the shop. Her pile of finished orders sat in the corner and grew. But none of their new owners had come to claim them—though a few had come to blatantly reject them and berate her for being dishonest. As a new business owner, she had already been struggling to gain footing in the town, especially after the fight. But now? Now she didn't know if she would be able to make her payments to Mr. Dallas for the month. More frustrations bubbled in her chest. Her landlord had already made it abundantly clear that he didn't think she could make it in business as an unmarried woman.

She hoped that if people saw her work with Beth's dress, it would help bring customers back. But thinking about the upcoming marriage brought her thoughts back to Boone. Kate wondered how she was going to keep avoiding him before the wedding. It was only three weeks away, but he seemed determined to see her. And though she was still angry about his deception, she still cared for him. Deeply. Annoyingly.

Kate's thoughts continued in the same pattern until eventually, the shop darkened. She considered working by lamplight, but her eyes were weary. She knew there would be no choice but to redo everything if she continued working now. Not bothering to tidy up—no one would see it anyway—Kate closed her shop and began walking home.

In the darkness, she imagined Mr. Dixon lurking in the shadows of every building. She'd grown accustomed to holding Boone's arm and having light conversations.

Stop it, Kate, she thought to herself. *You can walk home without an escort.*

She began walking briskly, but the sensation of someone watching her grew in intensity. She turned to check whether there was someone there, and she was positive she had seen a disappearing shadow. Quickening her pace, she ran home, threw the door open, and rushed through it. She slammed it behind her and locked it.

"Good. You're home," Charlotte said, sitting in the parlor. Seeing Kate so flushed, she asked, "Did Boone not walk you home?"

"What? Of course not. Why do you ask?"

Just then, Kate heard someone jiggle the door handle behind her and then knock brusquely. Sending Charlotte a concerned look, Kate asked through the door, "Who is it?"

"It's me, Kate. Open the door." Boone's impatient voice boomed. Steeling herself against the unavoidable interaction, Kate unlocked the door and moved out of the way just as Boone burst through. He removed his hat and raked his hand through his dark hair. His eyes stared at her and seemed to flood with a potent mixture of irritation and longing.

Boone appeared even more powerful and imposing to her in that moment. She nearly threw caution to the wind and ran into his embrace. The impulse was so strong, and she didn't know how to fight it, so she hitched up her skirts and bolted from the room, causing Charlotte to jolt in surprise.

Somehow, Kate managed to scurry up the stairs, get into her room, and shut the door. A knock told her that he'd come after her.

"Kate, please let me explain. Will you come out and talk with me?" he asked in clipped tones, his voice slightly muffled through the door.

"You have nothing to say that I want to hear, Mr. Carson," she said.

Kate heard him chuckle humorlessly then heard more footsteps coming up the stairs.

"Boone!" Charlotte was whispering loudly to him. "This boarding house is home to more than just the two of you, and some are trying to sleep. Kindly take your argument downstairs or stop altogether."

The hallway was quiet, and Kate put her ear to the door. She jumped slightly when she heard a soft knock on the other side.

"I just need a few minutes. You don't even need to talk. Will you please come downstairs and just listen?" Boone's voice was softer, more pleading, but Kate didn't care.

"No."

He exhaled sharply. "You sure are stubborn, Kit."

"Miss Morrison."

He pounded the door once in frustration. "Like I said. Stubborn."

Kate listened as his footsteps thumped down the stairs.

"Ugh! He is infuriating!" Kate hissed. She started pacing at the foot of her bed, too worked up to sleep. *I should have stayed at the shop.*

A thought struck her then. The shop! It wasn't Mr. Dixon who had been following and watching her—it had been Boone. It had to have been. Why else would he have come home only moments after she locked the door?

On an impulse, she ran down the stairs. She passed Charlotte, who sat in the parlor mending an apron.

"Kate, what are you doing?" she asked.

Without answering her, Kate rapped on Boone's door sharply.

"Kate?" Charlotte asked, looking very confused.

Kate turned to her. "I just need to ask him something," she said. Behind her, she heard the door open. She spoke as she turned around.

"Mr. Carson, did you or did you not..." She choked on the rest of the words when she found him standing there with his shirt unbuttoned, his impressive chest partially exposed.

"Boone Carson!" Charlotte scolded him from the couch. "Button up!" The tight line of Boone's lips softened into a smirk as he began to fasten his shirt.

Awash with tingles, Kate stepped back and looked everywhere except at him.

He grinned at her obvious discomfort and slowed his fingers. "Did you change your mind about listening to me?"

Her eyes snapped back to him, then darted away just as fast. "Um...no. I needed to ask you something."

"I see." He seemed pensive for a moment. "I'll make you a deal."

She fidgeted, unsure whether she should agree to anything he suggested.

"I'll answer your question as long as you listen to what I need to explain to you." He folded his arms, leaving the last three buttons undone.

Kate frowned. She was positive in her assumption that Boone had followed her home. But Beth's advice to listen to his full story came to her mind. Reluctantly, she nodded. "Deal."

He extended his hand. "I have your word? You *promise* that you'll hear me out?"

Kate took a large breath. He had emphasized the word *promise*, reminding her about the conversation they had on the subject a couple weeks ago. So, she resigned herself to listen to him, knowing that listening wasn't the same as believing or forgiving. She nodded once more. "I promise," she said as she returned his handshake. She wasn't prepared for the feeling of holding his hand again, and she tore hers away quickly.

Charlotte packed her mending bag. "I'd appreciate it if you didn't raise your voices," she said as she stood up and walked to the stairs. "I'll let you have this conversation in private, but please, have a sense of decorum and propriety!" She continued walking up to her room.

Boone fastened two more buttons, then walked to the couch. Kate followed, picking an armchair.

"What's your question, Kit?"

She folded her arms, her face tight. "Mr. Carson, I know you walked me home without my permission tonight."

He nodded. "That's not a question. And yeah, I did. And this morning too. Didn't want Dixon to find you alone," he said unapologetically, his expression serious.

"I have already told you to leave me alone. Your company is no longer needed or wanted."

He scoffed and leaned back. "I wasn't keeping you company. If anything, I was being a gentleman. Are you saying chivalry is no longer needed or wanted?"

Kate raised her chin. "Not by me."

"So, I should help everyone else in town except you?" He was glaring now.

"Yes! Or better yet, you should leave already and—"

"Listen here, Miss Uppity." Boone's voice started to rise, and he pointed his finger at Kate, emphasizing his next words. "I will continue to walk you to and from your shop while there's a scumbag like Dixon slithering around this town. You will either hold on to my arm, or I will follow you from the shadows. That's your choice. But your safety is more important to me than your pride!"

Kate was getting more riled up by the second. "You're saying I have no freedom anymore?" She waved her arms wildly. "You are my big, strong protector, and as long as I do what you say, everything will be just dandy?" she asked, her voice dripping with sarcasm. "And how do you plan to continue this demand after you go home and marry your sweetheart?" She was standing now, rage coursing through her veins. "I bet she has no idea what an untrustworthy, filthy philanderer she is bound to!"

"I wouldn't know!" he shouted, leaping to his feet. His expression twisted with rage, but Kate was shocked to see pain in his eyes as well.

A thick silence hung between them while their chests rose with angry breaths.

"What do you mean you wouldn't know?" Kate asked.

He sighed. "I wouldn't know because I've never met her."

"What?" Kate's confusion was complete, and she sat back down.

He sat as well and bowed his head. "I tried to tell you, but you didn't seem to hear me. And then you kicked me out before I could explain again."

She shook her head. "You said plenty. You said you were engaged."

"Yes." Boone looked at her. "But I didn't ask her. My parents did."

Kate sat for a moment while his words sunk in. "An arranged marriage?"

"Yes. That's what I was trying to tell you."

"Did they force you?" Kate couldn't hide the slight hope in her voice.

He shook his head with a grimace. "No. I asked for it."

Kate threw her hands up. "I guess that is that. You asked for something, and you got it. It's explained."

"No, it's not," Boone said in exasperation. "You promised to listen to me, so listen."

Kate pursed her lips but stopped talking.

Boone continued. "Before the war ended, I wrote to my mama and asked her to arrange a marriage for me. My mind was in a bad place, and I saw this as my only chance of a good life."

Kate scoffed, and he glared at her but kept going.

"I didn't know she'd accomplished my request until after I was healing from my wound."

A memory came to Kate's mind. "Is that why you asked me my opinion on arranged marriages? To see what you should do?"

"It was on my mind, and I...I didn't know whether I still wanted to go through with it."

"Why?"

He lifted his hands in exasperation. "Because of you! I admit I wanted to have an arranged marriage. But then I met you, and I changed my mind. I don't want it anymore, and I've been trying to write to my mama to cancel it."

Kate was dumbfounded, but her anger and hurt were still boiling up inside her. "How quickly you change your mind about your future wife. I wonder how fast it would change again if I were to fall for your tricks."

"That's not the same thing, Kate."

"Miss Morrison."

Boone groaned and raked his hands through his hair. "You are infuriating. I never changed my feelings from her to you because I had never felt anything for her. I've never met her, remember?"

Kate took a breath. "And what about *her*?"

"What do you mean?"

"Do you know what she thinks of this arrangement? Of you? Does she want this? Or is she being forced?" Hope glimmered in Kate's chest at the possibility that she might be able to accept his answer, but it would depend on the woman's response.

He looked away, as if he didn't want to answer. "After the conversation with you about arranged marriages, I asked my mama that very question. I wanted to know if my intended was forced into this arrangement and if she was, I could cancel the whole thing guilt-free. The day I told you about being technically engaged was the day I received my mama's answer." Boone reluctantly pulled out a letter from his pocket, opened it, and read a bit out loud.

...she tells us she is thrilled with the upcom-ing union and looks forward to meeting her future husband as soon as he is able to come back from his friend's wedding...

Kate's sliver of hope faded away, and she nodded solemnly. "In that case, I offer my congratulations to you on your impending nuptials." She stood to leave.

"What? No. I don't want to marry this woman," Boone said, standing as well.

"But clearly she wants to marry you. She accepted the arrangement that you asked for. You started this, and now you must follow through. That is an agree-ment—a promise—and like I said, you should never break a promise. I refuse to be the reason you break the heart of this young lady all because you found someone different, someone who appealed to you."

Boone gave her a quizzical look. "That logic might work in business, but when it concerns the heart, you don't just choose what came first. You choose what feels right, and that arrangement no longer feels right to me."

"That doesn't matter. If you were to make just any declaration of affection, how could anyone trust you, knowing how easily you change your mind? I know I couldn't."

Boone flinched, but Kate kept talking. "No, you must go back home as soon as possible and accept the arrangement."

Boone stepped closer, his gaze intense. Kate's body sent a traitorous thrill through her.

"If I leave here and marry this woman, it wouldn't be fair to her. And I would be living a lie. I have no affection for her. Only you." He closed the gap between them and took her face in his hands. Kate's heart snapped. "Kit, my sweet Kit, I—"

"Stop," she said, just barely whispering the word before she turned and fled up the stairs to the safety of her room.

With tears blurring her vision, she locked the door before leaning against it and sliding to the floor in a puddle of quiet sobs. She heard Boone's footsteps and knew he was standing just outside her door.

She wouldn't face him. Not now. She knew she couldn't handle it. Her will to fight against her love for him was nonexistent, and she needed to protect herself. She determined again that she would spend every moment she could away from the boarding house. Away from Boone. She would sleep in her shop. Kate was willing to risk it until Mr. Dixon inevitably found out.

Kate crawled into her bed then, not bothering to change her clothes. She still loved Boone, and she was positive that he had almost professed his love for her. But despite all that, she couldn't trust that his affection was sincere. And even if he did genuinely love her, she couldn't let him hurt that faraway woman the same way that Henry had hurt Kate. These thoughts spun around in her head until she had no more tears left to cry.

The last thing she thought about before finally drifting to sleep was wondering whether Boone would leave her door. She had yet to hear any retreating footsteps.

Seventeen

A week later, Kate opened the boarding house door as quietly as possible. In an effort to avoid Boone, she'd been waking up before the sun, sneaking off to her shop, and not returning until late. Her meals were cold and sometimes stale, but she was determined to push through till Boone left and took his fickle heart with him.

Whenever he did catch her, he'd ask her to read another letter. She made every attempt to be polite each time she refused, but he was becoming more and more insistent. Her irritation would grow until, at the end of the day, her temper would explode and result in the same argument. While they tried to be civil in the boarding house, they soon learned that even that wasn't a foolproof way to avoid their heated disagreements.

She wished she could talk to Beth about the arguments, but she and Jesse had recently made friends with a newly married couple. Kate felt a pang of jealousy and wondered what it would be like if she and Boone were that other couple.

"Stop it," Kate said to herself—she was on an empty street. She didn't need Boone to be happy. She had finally achieved the freedom and independence that she'd wanted her entire life, and she wasn't about to give that up.

She forced herself to think of the people who had hurt her: Boone. Mother and Father. Henry. She scowled. They used me. They made me love them, and then they betrayed me.

Kate sighed as she unlocked her door and again reminded herself that Boone would be gone for good in less than three weeks.

Kate walked in and looked around. A few days ago, she had moved all the unclaimed orders into the small storage room at the back. Hiding the orders seemed to help motivate her to try and salvage something from Mr. Dixon's cruel attempts to ruin her business.

So, after hearing from Beth about all the new babies who had been born in the last month, she had decided to make Sunday outfits for each child. With each outfit, the people got to know her for who she really was and got to see her skills up close. Little by little, customers had again begun to trickle into her shop to request new commissions.

As Kate went about her work, a handful of people came to collect their orders. Most pretended nothing odd had happened, but a few apologized for listening to the gossip. While Kate knew she still had a lot of work to do to gain the trust of the town back, she felt a bit of hope for the first time since Boone had told her of his engagement.

The sun had been down for a while when Kate's stomach let her know that it ached from hunger and wasn't going to allow her to concentrate on anything else.

She cleaned up, locked the doors, and turned to walk home when she saw a shape sitting on the bottom step in front of her. She sighed in disgust.

"What do you want this time, Mr. Dixon?" She stood out of his reach by the door, and with the little light from the moon, she could clearly tell he was inebriated as he scrambled to his feet.

From her window, Kate had frequently seen Mr. Dixon and another man stumbling out of the saloon doors. Sometimes he'd come over to propose or to ask if she had changed her mind, and other times, he'd stare at her shop from across the street until the smaller man would pull him away. This time he was alone.

"I jus'...I wanna see...if ya changed yer mind. I bet yer almost broke." He let out a snort of humor. "Sort of." He belched and scratched his stomach, swaying slightly.

Kate rolled her eyes. "I don't see how that's any of your concern, Mr. Dixon," Kate said, folding her arms. She was positive she could outrun him in his current state.

"I'm jus' bein' a friendly neighbor."

"You've never been friendly to me. I've given you my answer, Mr. Dixon. Many times. I will never change my mind." She kept her voice level and controlled, but there was no one around, and she hoped Mr. Dixon wouldn't try anything rash.

Mr. Dixon's loose smile hardened into a sneer. He grabbed the railing and steadied himself. "Now ya listen to me, missy. I—"

"Evening, Miss Morrison, Dixon," Sheriff Garret said, riding down the street on his horse. Kate hadn't noticed him in the darkness.

"I need to speak with the lady in private, Dixon. Go home and sleep this off."

Mr. Dixon huffed but nodded and walked away.

After they lost sight of Mr. Dixon, Kate turned to the sheriff. "What did you need to speak with me about?"

"Nothin'," he said, his horse shifting slightly.

"What?"

"I've been keeping a closer eye on Dixon after that scuffle with Mr. Carson. He's been spending too much time in the saloon for my taste, and something about him don't sit right with me." The older man bowed his head. "I apologize for not believing ya that day, Miss Morrison. I still can't prove it or do anything about it, but I know you shouldn't be alone in Dixon's company."

"Thank you, Sheriff," Kate said.

"Now you run on home. I'm gonna stay here a while longer."

Kate nodded and left.

The boarding house was dark except for a single light shining through the parlor window. Kate smiled and opened the front door.

"Charlotte, you don't have to wait up for me." Kate said as she walked into the parlor. Someone was sitting in the armchair facing the embers in the hearth. But it wasn't Charlotte.

Boone stood and faced her. "Kate, I need you to read this letter." The pleading in his voice almost broke her. "Please. Then we need to talk." His deep blue eyes searched her face.

"Boone, stop. I can't do this." She wanted to run, but his eyes had arrested her.

Her heart pounded in her chest, emotion thick in her throat. He took a step toward her, but she moved back.

"I just don't understand," he said. "It's not a crime to ask your parents to arrange a marriage, but I didn't realize it was a mistake for me. I couldn't go through with it now, not after I met you." He took another step forward, his hand reaching for her. Kate shook her head slightly, and he let it drop back to his side.

"Well, you can't get out of it so easily!" Anger ripped through her like a tornado. "You asked for this, so this is what you are getting."

"Why do you keep saying that? I told you it's not what I want anymore."

"But you did, and some young woman out there is expecting you to marry her. You said yourself that she is excited, probably planning her future with you despite never having met you. Do you know how much you will crush her dreams? All because you changed your mind?" Kate was breathing hard, and heat flooded her body.

"We can't know all that for sure. I'm not trying to hurt her, but I refuse to be forced into something that I don't want. Why are you making me out to be the villain?" Boone's eyes were wide.

Kate scoffed. "Now you know what women have to deal with. Arranged marriages are usually just a form of control. Daughters must marry someone their parents approve of." Her hand flew into the air, and she took a step toward him. "But men get to say when, who, or if they even want to marry." Kate was now right in front of Boone, her gaze locked on his face. "How do you think it feels to have your life manipulated and then dictated to you? How do you think it feels to believe someone loves you and wants to marry you, and then you find out they changed their mind?" She wanted to shove him—make him feel the pain she had felt. "How long will her broken heart last?" Kate looked away quickly and let her gaze drop. She hadn't meant to talk about herself.

Boone's eyes narrowed, and he stared at her. "You're hiding something from me." She closed her eyes and shook her head. "Will you tell me?"

"No." She ducked around him and walked away. She couldn't tell him. *He is leaving.*

He turned toward her. "What's the worst that could happen by telling me the truth?"

She shook her head again. *I'd give you the rest of my heart, and you'd still leave.*

"Kate! Look at me," he said. She tried to ignore the way her name sounded on his lips. "You're shutting me out for no reason!" he shouted.

She stopped and put her hands over her ears to block everything out. Her painful past, her broken future—all the things that had been building inside her for the past two years.

"Just tell me what happened!" She could hear him through her hands, and she lowered them.

She stopped. The silence that followed filled the parlor more than Boone's shouting had. Slowly she turned around and looked at him. He seemed so completely lost. For a moment, Kate almost felt sorry for him. Instead, she lifted her chin and stared at him, trying to determine if he was telling the truth or just saying what she wanted to hear.

"You owe me a truthful explanation, Miss Kit," he said, glowering at her. "No more skirting around it. It's time to tell me what's going on in that beautiful, fool head of yours."

Kate's voice turned cold. "I owe you? You sure seem to want a lot of things, Mr. Carson! You want a reason?'"

Despite her normal volume, Boone looked even more stunned than before. *Good,* she thought and continued.

"You will never know the hurt I have known at the hands of people who thought they knew what was best for me! Nobody has ever asked what I wanted! Not you. Not my mother! Certainly not Lez Dixon! And not Henry!" Kate got more heated as she listed each person, her hands flying with every name.

Boone just stood there, his arms crossed over his chest. He never took his eyes off her, but to his credit, he kept his mouth shut.

Kate started pacing and continued her tirade. "I didn't get a say about a marriage with Henry. Not until I met him. He was charming and sweet, and he seemed completely devoted to me. For the first time, my thoughts lined up with my mother's." Kate's scowl deepened. "But after a few months, I learned that he didn't love me at all. He only loved the money my mother bribed him with, but even that wasn't enough. He started pursuing an heiress and threw me aside." Kate froze. *I can't believe I just said all that out loud.*

Boone held up his hands, getting Kate's attention. "You're hurt because he betrayed you by backing out of an arrangement that you wanted. I get it. But clearly, he didn't want it. You told me that if one person doesn't want the arrangement, then a marriage shouldn't happen. So why does mine have to?"

Kate's anger flared again. "You are infuriating! I know what it's like to be on the other side of your situation." Kate pointed her finger at Boone. "In your circumstance, I've become the heiress—the woman I hated for taking Henry away from me. I refuse to be the cause of that other woman's heartache. I loved Henry, and I wish he had honored our agreement."

Boone sighed, but Kate continued. "But he would not. And nobody cared that I was crushed. A few months after Henry broke his connection with me, I discovered Mother had arranged yet another marriage. I would not fall into another trap like that. Never again. So, I left home and fled as far as my own hard-earned money would take me."

"To Brexton," Boone said softly.

Kate crossed her arms. "Yes. And then I met you. Against my better judgment, I got to know you and grew to care for you—a man I knew was going to go back home in a month. Why did you think I would want to share my greatest pain with you?" She stopped pacing, her arms wrapped tightly around herself. His frown deepened, but he said nothing.

"I'm right back where I started. Betrayed again. And both times were because of an arranged marriage." Kate watched Boone's brow furrow into a scowl. "Is that enough of an explanation for you, Mr. Carson?"

Without waiting for a response, Kate turned on her heel and left the boarding house to go straight to her shop. She had arranged for a cot to be put in the back room should she need to stay late. As she lay down to try and sleep, she entertained the thought of staying in her shop until Boone left.

Boone stood there, slowly processing the barrage of information Kate had slung at him. Part of him had wanted to argue with her conflicting logic, but a wiser part of him knew to stay quiet and let her rant. And how grateful he was that he had listened. As bits of her past came to light, his own dismay grew.

What he had learned sent his own emotions through a whirlwind. He was angry that she'd compared him to this scoundrel Henry. But he was curious—this was the most she had ever shared with him about her past. It hadn't really mattered to him since he'd gotten to know her, but he wanted to know more about the life she'd led before.

His blood boiled as he thought about how Henry had hurt Kate. *Yet, she still loved him then. Why can't she love me now?* Boone raked his hands through his hair and groaned as he realized how the untimely news of his arranged marriage had sounded to her. She had thought the past was repeating itself, and the guilt weighed heavily on his heart.

However, his heart had surged when Kate had talked about growing to care for him. Her words had been enough to give him hope, and he was determined to continue trying to prove his devotion to her. The letter he ached to give her seemed to burn in his pocket.

He chuckled wryly as he remembered how Kate had ripped and drowned the first one. She had to know that he was serious, and so he had written a second letter, then he had written a copy to send to his mama.

The first he kept in his pocket should he ever get the chance to give it to Kate—if he could get Kate to actually read it, Boone was positive he could convince her of his love.

Even if Kate seemed to have made up her mind, Boone was determined to keep trying.

"But how?" he asked the empty parlor.

I need to talk to Charlotte.

Not waiting another moment, he sprinted up the stairs and knocked on her door.

"Charlotte! I need your advice!" he whispered.

She opened the door immediately. "Boone, what's wrong?" she asked, her eyes wide with concern.

"I don't know what to do."

"Let's talk in the parlor," Charlotte said, walking with him.

They sat in the armchairs, and Boone launched into his thoughts. "I might lose the woman I love, and I need your help."

Charlotte's mouth fell open, and she let out a small gasp. "Wait...are you talking about Kate?" she asked after she regained her composure.

"Yes. I love Kate, but she won't listen to me long enough for me to tell her. And I don't think she'd believe me at this point anyway."

Charlotte let out a heavy stream of air. "Tell me what happened."

Boone didn't go into details, unsure of what Kate wanted others to know.

"I messed up real bad Charlotte, though I had no idea this would happen. Kate's been hurt. Hurt bad by people, including her mother, who have tried to control her life with arranged marriages. That's why she's here, and why she doesn't trust me. She doesn't want to hurt someone else the way she was hurt." He looked at Charlotte for a moment, but she was quiet, so he continued. "Now she won't let me break my arrangement, and I don't know how to change her mind." He finished in a rush.

Charlotte turned to him and asked, "Do you know how she feels about you?"

Boone's shoulders drooped. "I know that at one point she cared for me. I can't tell you whether she feels the same now. Besides, she left a few minutes ago. I'm assuming she decided to sleep at her shop to avoid me." He looked up at Charlotte once more, pleading to her with his eyes. "What can I do? How can I get her to listen to me?" He removed the letter from his pocket. "If she would just read this letter, I know it would clear everything up."

Charlotte thought for a moment before taking Boone's hand in her own and patting the back of it sweetly. "It seems to me that you are doin' the very thing she ran away from home to avoid."

Boone's brow furrowed.

Charlotte sighed. "You're not lettin' her decide for herself. You're tryin' to force her to listen to you: 'Kate, read this letter. Kate, listen to me. Kate, do as I say.'"

Understanding washed over Boone. Charlotte was right. He had been pushing Kate to do things his way without giving her a choice. No wonder she kept running from him.

"Then what should I do?" he asked.

"Don't back her into a corner. If you truly love her, give her the letter and then walk away. Let her decide what to do, and once she does, respect that decision, no matter what it might do to your heart."

Boone hung his head again, and Charlotte put a hand on his shoulder.

But what if Kate doesn't choose me? Boone couldn't bear the thought.

Eighteen

Kate lay in the cot for an hour after she'd arrived, but sleep wouldn't come. She tried to blame it on the hardness of the bed beneath her, but she knew it was because of Boone. It bothered her how much she'd told him. She prayed it would be enough to convince him to leave her alone until he left town.

A knock came from the back door only a few feet from her cot, and Kate sucked in a breath. Was it Mr. Dixon? Boone? She didn't want to deal with either man, so she stayed as still as possible, hoping they would go away.

"Kate, it's me. Open up," came a muffled, feminine voice.

"Charlotte?" Kate stood up and hurried to the door, unlocking it and letting her in.

"I apologize if I woke ya," Charlotte said.

"No. I haven't been able to fall asleep yet," Kate said as she lit a lantern to fill the darkness.

Quiet fell between them for a moment while Charlotte watched her. The older woman's eyes seemed to be searching for something unspoken.

Kate sighed. "Why are you here?"

Charlotte gave her a pointed look. "You must be thick in the head, Kate. Boone told me where you went, and I came to make sure you were all right."

Kate was warmed by the gesture. Her mother had rarely checked on her well-being. "Thank you for coming. I just needed to...to have some space."

Charlotte nodded. "I told Boone to go to bed and stay there till mornin', but I'm not comfortable with you stayin' here by yourself. Especially with Mr. Dixon around."

"I appreciate your concern, but I saw him earlier this evening. I wouldn't be surprised if he is unconscious from all the liquor he drank tonight. He could barely stand straight, and the sheriff already sent him home."

"That does soothe my heart somewhat, but I'm still worried about ya. Do you want to talk about what happened tonight with Boone?" Charlotte asked, taking Kate's hand.

Kate shook her head. "Not tonight. I need to think about some things. Maybe tomorrow?" She hoped Charlotte would forget to bring it up.

Charlotte nodded and pulled Kate into a warm hug. "Very well. Be safe, dear. I'll come by in the mornin' with some breakfast." She got up and was gone as quickly as she'd arrived.

Something about Charlotte's concern brought a measure of peace to Kate's mind, and she suddenly felt tired.

She climbed back onto the cot, and the last thought she had before falling asleep was about Boone.

As soon as Kate awoke the next morning, her mind started replaying her debate with Boone. Her thoughts lingered on what Boone had said about her and Henry.

"Clearly, he didn't want it. You told me that if one person doesn't want the arrangement, then a marriage shouldn't happen. So why does mine have to?"

His words looped through her mind until she thought she would go mad. She wished she had said something different. That she hadn't told him so much. But now he knew, and she didn't want to be the one to hurt this poor woman who was promised to Boone. Was there another reason? Searching for another answer to that question resulted only in frustration. None of her potential answers seemed like a good enough reason.

Confound it, Boone, she thought as she got out of her cot abruptly. Henry hadn't loved her, but she had wanted him to follow through with the marriage anyway—all because she wanted it. Why? She closed her eyes and tried to imagine what her life would be like if Henry hadn't broken the engagement. Would he have learned to love her, or would he have betrayed her in the end? When she opened her eyes, she felt more unsure than ever.

She freshened herself up and prepared for the day until she heard a knock at the front door and Charlotte's voice coming through the wood.

"Good morning, Kate," Charlotte said. Kate unlocked the door, and Charlotte walked in holding a delicious-smelling basket. "Did you sleep well? Or at least sleep?"

Kate chuckled. "I slept better than I thought I would."

"Wonderful. You eat up, and then we'll talk about last night."

Kate sighed. So much for Charlotte forgetting.

She forced a smile. "I don't think we need to talk about it. I'll be fine. I just needed to stay here to...air out a...a certain... frustration."

"I know the feeling," Charlotte said as she placed the basket on an empty chair. "When I was your age, I had a certain frustration too."

"How did you fix it?"

Charlotte heaved a deep sigh. "Well, I never fixed it. But I did marry it, and that seemed to clear up a few issues." Both women chuckled. "Mind you, marriage didn't do away with all the bad, but it did make the good that much better," the older woman said, sitting down.

"Charlotte, I can't—"

Charlotte held her hand up. "I ain't here to tell you what to do. All I know is, somethin' in your heart is hurtin' and has been since before you met Boone." Charlotte's gaze was direct.

Kate lifted her chin. "Boone told you everything, didn't he?"

Charlotte shrugged. "Not everything. Actually, not much at all. But from the little he said, it sounds like you've had a rough go of it."

Kate looked away, biting the inside of her cheek and taking a deep breath. She wasn't sure she could get through saying it all again. But when she looked at Charlotte, she saw nothing but concern in her eyes. Maybe it was a good thing that someone else knew.

Charlotte patted the chair next to her. "Boone only told me a little. Would you be willing to share the rest of your story with me?"

Kate paused but then sighed and sat next to Charlotte. She kept her back straight and her head held high. "My experience with love has been..." Kate stopped and closed her eyes briefly.

"Has been what, dear?" Charlotte's eyes were kind but observant. Kate knew she had many questions. But words wouldn't come, and Kate looked away.

Charlotte sighed. When Kate looked up, Charlotte was looking at Kate with the most motherly expression—it made her want to weep. Charlotte turned and took Kate by the shoulders. "Kate, if you can't be honest with me, then you need to be honest with yourself and with Boone—especially about why you're upset with him. I'm here to listen to you and help you with whatever you may need. All I ask is that you be honest about what you want in life. Really, truly, and sincerely honest."

"I just want to be left alone so I can be happy." Kate's voice quivered.

"You think being alone is going to make you happy?" Charlotte straightened, her eyebrow raised.

"It's better than being hurt again and again." Kate looked at her hands, lying perfectly still in her lap.

"Kate, I've been on this earth for a few years. I know the pain life can bring." Kate looked up and saw tears glistening in her eyes. "I used to be married and had three sons and two daughters. My husband left me after our oldest daughter died. It was a terrible accident, and my husband blamed himself. I was alone when sickness claimed my other daughter and my youngest son. Each loss threatened to consume me. The war took my eldest son. Jesse is the only one I have left, and I fight every day for him."

Kate's mouth dropped open in shock. She took the older woman's hand and squeezed it.

"I am so sorry, Charlotte." She couldn't find the words.

Charlotte cleared her throat, "Many times I wanted to give up and die, but I've always hoped for a brighter future, and now," she smiled, "I get to see my son wed a wonderful woman. One whom I have grown to love and care for like my own daughter. I want you to be open to the happiness you could find with Boone."

"How can you still believe in that kind of happiness?" Kate tried to swallow the lump in her throat.

"I realized years ago that we wouldn't be able to appreciate the good without knowin' the hard times. Life teaches us important lessons through such times."

"I hope I become as strong and wise as you someday," Kate said, giving Charlotte a weak smile.

"You're already strong. And wisdom comes with age and experience. Till you get more of that, you can borrow mine," Charlotte chuckled, wiping her tears.

They were silent for a time. Kate thought about her own story. Fear and the truth battled within her heart. *Would it really help me to share my story? What's the worst that could happen?*

Kate opened her mouth, and everything spilled from her lips.

"When I was 17, my mother arranged a marriage for me with a man named Henry Weston. He was from a wealthy family. Mother thought he was a perfect match, but I hated the whole arrangement. But when he came over to meet me, he was charming and handsome, and I found myself wanting to be around him. We courted for four months while our parents planned the wedding. He said he loved me, and I thought I had fallen in love with him too." Kate sighed, and her heart pounded in her chest as she hugged herself.

"The wedding preparations were nearly finished when Henry suddenly stopped coming to see me. Mother became increasingly agitated and sent as many letters out as I did. Two weeks before the wedding, Henry sent a short note telling me that he was calling off the wedding and that he would no longer be accepting bribes from my mother."

Charlotte gasped, and Kate nodded, her eyes burning at the memory. "He had been cut off when his family found out about his gambling debts, so he had decided to pursue a wealthy heiress. Apparently, my mother's continued bribes weren't enough anymore. I wasn't enough. But he never loved me, did he? Everything between us had been a lie."

Charlotte shook her head "Kate, I'm so sorry. I'm sorry your mother and this man betrayed you in such a way."

"That's not the end." Kate hung her head. "After that betrayal, I became more serious about becoming a seamstress. I wanted to be independent and figure out my life, but that wasn't good enough for my mother. She wanted me married off and controlled."

Charlotte huffed in frustration.

"She secretly put an advertisement in the paper, but I found it." Kate's hands contracted into fists as she recited the memorized words. "'Seeking a wealthy man in want of a lovely, socialite bride who comes with a sizable dowry. Able to marry at your earliest convenience. Young lady is 18 years old, healthy, and knows how to run a well-to-do household. No age requirements for any inquiring gentleman should he meet the previous requirements.'"

Kate could hear Charlotte's angry breathing.

"My mother was so determined to marry me off, she would accept any old geezer." Kate buried her face in her hands. "It wasn't long after that that I heard my mother telling my father a new man had been found. She said I wouldn't have time to get to know the gentleman since he was away on business and would be for some time. She said we would be married the week after he arrived home."

Kate shook her head in disbelief. "I can't believe she could think I would ever trust an arranged marriage after what happened with Henry.

"Not only did she arrange another one, but she did so with a complete stranger that I wouldn't have time to get to know before we were married. So, I bought a train ticket that night with the money I'd been saving by taking on projects as a seamstress. I couldn't let Mother control and manipulate my life any longer. When I arrived in Albuquerque, I heard Brexton was a good place to settle. So here I am."

Charlotte let out a long breath. "That's a lot to take in," she said. "I can understand why you're upset with Boone's news."

Kate felt so much relief knowing that Charlotte agreed with her. "I am upset. Boone is breaking his engagement just as Henry broke his."

Charlotte paused and looked at Kate with an uncertain look.

"What is it?" Kate asked.

"I'm sorry Kate, it's just...Boone's situation sounds completely different than the one with this Henry."

"What?" Kate said, shocked.

"You fell in love with Henry. You formed an attachment to him despite the arrangement. And you thought he loved you. But with Boone's arrangement, they've never met. Boone didn't make this woman think he loved her. Even if she is excited about it, I can't imagine her heart would be crushed if it was canceled like yours was. It's not fair to make Boone responsible for that."

"No, that's not...Didn't you listen to my story?"

"I did. Did you?"

Kate's mouth dropped open in disbelief, but Charlotte took her hands before she could speak. "Kate Morrison, I want you to answer this question. Don't tell me, just think about this." Charlotte paused, and Kate listened intently, though she was still shocked at Charlotte's response.

"What do you want in life? Open your heart and mind, and maybe what you discover will surprise you." Charlotte lifted Kate's chin. "Figure out what *you* want, Kate, then fight for it with everythin' you have."

Charlotte hugged Kate and turned to leave. She stopped at the door and looked over her shoulder. "Thank you for tellin' me the truth. I know it isn't easy. You're a strong woman, Kate, but even a strong woman should know when to ask for help." Then she left, leaving a stunned Kate alone in the shop.

Nineteen

The next two days passed without any interaction between Kate and Boone, and the few times they were together were tense and awkward. Kate had taken to sleeping at her shop nearly every night. Occasionally, Boone would approach her with his letter in hand, but another patron always seemed to enter the room at the same time, giving Kate a chance to escape.

While Kate knew Boone wanted to talk with her, she did notice that he no longer made demands, tried to argue with her, or tried to force her to listen to him. Even though she was positive it would end only in heartbreak for her, she secretly wished for another argument to erupt between them just so they could talk. All of these contradictory thoughts confused her, and she wondered if she was still in her right mind.

Charlotte hadn't said another word regarding their earlier discussion, but each time they were together, she would stare at Kate, a question in her eyes. Each time, Kate would shake her head.

Kate had been pondering the things her friends had said to her. Beth and Charlotte had both tried to convince her that Boone's feelings for Kate were genuine and true, unlike Henry's pretended feelings. Kate was starting to think she had been wrong to compare Boone to Henry. But she just didn't know if she was ready to trust Boone with her heart.

What made it worse was that despite everything, Kate still loved Boone— a stronger love than she'd ever felt for Henry. She wondered if he felt the same for her. He had never said as much, but his actions lead her to believe that he at least cared deeply for her. But what about his letter? Would it confirm her fears or get rid of them entirely?

But each night as she drifted to sleep, Kate allowed herself to hope that Boone, Charlotte, and Beth were right—that his feelings were sincere, and that breaking his previous engagement wouldn't crush the tender heart of some faraway young heiress.

Kate would fall asleep with hope in her heart, but doubt would always fill it the minute she awoke. She counted down the days till Boone left so she could begin to heal—or at least try to.

When Sunday came and Kate couldn't distract herself with the shop, she resigned herself to spending a tense morning avoiding Boone. It was nearly noon, and she'd managed to avoid him all morning during church. She now worked with Charlotte to prepare lunch, and the sweet smell of the cornbread they had made was almost enough to distract her from her worries.

"I'm finished with the bacon, Charlotte. Is there anything else you need help with?"

"The cornbread is almost done. I'll put this pie in, and it can bake while we eat," Charlotte said as she pinched the edges of a pie crust. "I suppose you could you fetch Jesse from the barn now. He promised he would fix that railing on the porch before he ate lunch."

"Sure," Kate said, smiling as she left.

Kate kept a wary eye out for Boone and relaxed when she didn't see him. Hopefully, he was in town on some errand. But as she approached the slightly open barn doors, she heard the voices of Jesse and Boone coming from inside. Kate stopped abruptly. She started to decide what excuse to give Charlotte for not getting Jesse when she heard her name. Part of her knew it was unwise, but she had to know what they were saying about her.

Creeping closer, the voices became clearer, and Kate heard a third voice, higher than the others.

Beth? she wondered. *What is she doing here?*

"What else have you tried?" Kate heard Jesse say.

"You could try cornering her again," Beth said. "She might be angry at first, but she needs to know." Kate leaned even closer, shocked her friend would suggest such a thing.

"No, I won't force her to listen to me," Boone said emphatically. "She's been bullied and pushed around enough. I refuse to do that to her." His voice filled with dejection then. "I've tried everything I can think of to get her to talk to me, but she won't even look at me." Kate jumped as she heard something solid hit the wall.

"How's that even possible? You live in the same house," Beth said.

Boone gave a wry laugh. "That woman is an expert in avoiding me. If she can't leave the room before I get there, someone else always comes in. I'm beginning to think Kate set up these interruptions with the other patrons. I thought I had her on the staircase yesterday, but she still slipped past me without so much as a glance in my direction."

Kate shivered as she remembered the incident. She'd nearly thrown her arms around him as he whispered to her, pleading with her to talk to him for just a minute. She had to remind herself that even if he didn't want the arrangement anymore, he was technically promised to another woman.

"You've gotta talk to her. She needs to know what you've told us." Jesse's words brought Kate back to the conversation.

"You think I don't know that? I know I can't force her, but I'm stepping on glass trying to say the right thing to get her to listen. It's driving me crazy! I'd rather start an argument with her 'cause at least that way, we'd be talking!"

Kate's heart fluttered at his words. Knowing he felt the same way about talking again strangely comforted her. Tiptoeing around each other was having a worse effect on her than their fighting had ever had.

Boone started talking again. "I just need Kate to hear me out. She's misunderstood my thoughts and feelings, and she's put her thorns up. If I could just get her to stay still and listen—really listen without jumping down my throat—I know I could clear this up. I know it."

The trio fell silent. Kate held her breath, desperate to not miss anything.

"What would you tell her?" Beth asked softly.

Kate felt a tug on her heart to hear what he was planning to say to her, but Boone didn't answer. Frustrated, Kate wanted to call out for him to speak up, but she held her tongue. She dared to peek around the partially open door to see what kept him silent.

As her gaze focused on the scene in the barn, she saw Boone sitting on a stool, his elbows resting on his knees with his face in his hands— miserable, dejected, and tired. Kate pushed away the urge to sooth his ache, knowing it would only add to her own.

Beth and Jesse were looking at their friend and then at each other, their brows creased with worry. Finally, Boone looked up and Kate's breath caught at the sight of him, the love she felt simultaneously filling and breaking her heart.

Slowly, he reached into his pocket. It was the letter he'd been asking her to read for the last week.

"I would tell her—ask her to read this letter, and if she agrees, I'd leave her to do so and decide for herself. Every word is the truth, and if she still can't accept that..." Boone paused and rubbed his face in frustration. "If she still wants nothing to do with me, then I'll stop trying. For good."

A whimpering cry escaped her lips at the thought of never seeing him again. Much to her humiliation, all three heads turned in her direction.

For the briefest of moments, Boone's gaze locked with hers. He leapt to his feet and stepped toward her, but fear and instinct made her whirl around and sprint away.

"Kate!"

She didn't stop or turn. She just kept running.

"Kate, stop!"

When she reached the front of the house, she turned left and took the street that led out of Brexton. She couldn't face Boone. Or Charlotte, or Beth. She couldn't deal with the people in town or Mr. Dixon's leering gaze. She didn't want to think about her past or her future. So at the bend in the road, she ran into the desert. She ran toward nothing with only the sound of her labored breathing and the pounding of her heart in her ears.

She didn't know if Boone was coming after her, but she kept moving. Her heart hoped he would chase after her but her head hoped he would leave her alone.

Her lungs burned, and her legs began to ache, but she pushed the pain aside. And then, in a moment of clarity, she realized that she was doing what she had always done.

She was running away—again.

Her embarrassment for being caught eavesdropping paled in comparison to her fear of the contents of Boone's letter. What if she decided to believe him and he stayed? What if she rejected him and he left? What if she was right and he was exactly like Henry? Each thought terrified her.

After going for what felt like miles, her body screaming for reprieve, Kate finally stopped running. Taking in great gulps of air, she realized she hadn't heard any sound of Boone. He would have caught her by now if he had chased her. The thought was both disappointing and pleasing, which she couldn't understand.

At the sound of hoofbeats, she turned around to see Boone a few yards away, riding his horse bareback. When he slowed to a stop, his gaze was powerful and fierce, but he said nothing.

Kate felt foolish, but whether it was from running or seeing Boone, she couldn't tell. Her face burned, and she hoped it would pass as the flush from running instead of from the truth of her feelings for him. She didn't want to look at him, but he looked so imposing that she couldn't tear her eyes away.

They stood there, staring at one another, while a million thoughts raced through Kate's mind: thoughts about Boone and the conflicting feelings she had for him as well as thoughts that wondered about what he felt for her. She thought about her past, and her fight for her own independence despite her mother's intentions. Those thoughts and so many more raced through her mind until a headache formed, but still, Kate couldn't speak or move.

As she wrestled with the chaos in her mind, Charlotte's loving advice came to the front, and the rest of her thoughts quieted.

Be honest with yourself, and figure out what you want.

One by one the thoughts in her mind began to settle, and what she wanted became clear.

Kate wanted Boone Carson. She wanted him to be the biggest part of her life. She wanted him to be her husband. She wanted to build a life and a family together. And despite her fears and the hurt in her heart, she loved him. And there he was, right in front of her—watching and waiting.

As this new fear coursed through her body, her original fears doubled. She did want him, but she still didn't know whether she could trust him to not break her heart.

Kate squared her shoulders and lifted her chin, hoping it gave her the confidence she was sorely lacking. Boone raised one eyebrow, but she ignored it.

"Mr. Carson, I would appreciate it if you left me alone. We've decided that, given the current situation, our spending time together would be unacceptable."

Boone said nothing. Without looking away, he nudged his horse in the side and moved closer. He stopped a few feet from her. He folded his arms in front of his chest. "We didn't decide anything, Miss Kit. You did."

Kate huffed. "For the last time. It is Miss Morrison. And I didn't think you could be trusted any longer, Mr. Carson."

He gave her a look that nearly turned her knees to jelly. "The way I figure it, Miss Kit, is that you don't trust me because you haven't listened to me. I've tried to be respectful of your feelings, but you need to know certain things."

Kate squirmed. "I already know what I need to know about you."

"No, you don't." He pulled the letter from his pants again. "I've been patient with you Kate." She scoffed, and Boone chuckled dryly. "And maybe a little stubborn. But when I tried to explain myself to you, you took the first words that tumbled out of my mouth and made your mind up about something that ain't true. This letter," he shook it, "will tell you exactly where I stand. All I ask is that you read it, think on it, then come talk to me."

Kate eyed the paper in his hand for a moment. She was terrified about what it might say, yet she found herself itching to find out. "And what good will that do? You're leaving anyway."

He shook his head. "I ain't leaving, Kit."

"Yes, you are. You're going to go home and get...married." She choked on the last word. Why couldn't she let this go? It was clear that Boone was getting frustrated. Even she had to admit this conversation was going in the same circle.

He looked her in the eye, his stare so intense that Kate took a step back. "Kate, if I leave here, it will be because I know without a doubt that I'm not wanted. But I won't know that till you read this letter and make your decision." Kate's heart started pounding faster than it had when she was running.

Boone held the letter down to her. "Now, I wanted to hash this out together, but I didn't think you'd believe me. So, this is a copy of a letter I wrote to my mama, and I've already sent that one. She might even have it by now."

Kate grew more intrigued about what he'd written.

"I need you to know I'm serious. I'll leave you alone so you can sit with it and think. Would you do that?"

Kate's heart thundered in her chest. Her unease must have shown on her face because Boone dismounted in one smooth motion and walked slowly to her.

"I know you're unsure about this. Maybe even scared. But I promise you, if you will read it and ponder it, I'll abide by whatever you decide."

She watched him, his eyes clear and intent. The battle between her heart and mind grew fierce. She peered at the letter, half expecting it to bite her. Finally, her heart won, and she nodded. "I'll read it."

Boone's eyes widened. "Really? You will?"

"Yes." The look of surprise on Boone's face nearly made her chuckle.

His eyes narrowed slightly. "Are you *actually* going to read it or just drown it like you did the last one?"

Kate blushed. "I will read it and give it back to you in one piece. You have my word."

After a moment, he nodded. "And you'll talk with me when you're ready?"

Kate nodded.

"Very well," he said, apparently satisfied with her response. He handed her the letter and mounted his horse again. "Do you want a ride back to town?"

Kate looked back to the town and realized she hadn't run as far as she'd thought. "No, but thank you for offering."

Boone looked at her, and she knew he wanted to argue. But he held his tongue and expelled a deep sigh. "Very well. I'll leave you alone now."

She nodded; grateful he was listening to her wishes. It was a refreshing change from what she'd grown up with. He clicked his tongue and rode away toward the boarding house.

Her heart pounded to the sound of the horse retreating. She turned the letter over and over in her hands. She wondered what Boone could have said to his mother that gave him the confidence to say he could change Kate's mind.

As she passed the boarding house, she saw two men stumbling out of the saloon. Kate could tell it was Mr. Dixon and the stranger he was often with now. They ambled around the corner. They were walking toward her shop, but Mr. Dixon's property was down this street as well, so Kate wasn't worried. Since most stores closed on Sundays, Mr. Dixon was likely to simply pass by the shop, so she kept walking. Sure enough, when she turned the corner and saw her shop, Mr. Dixon and his companion were down the road, staggering home.

After one last look to make sure Mr. Dixon was indeed going home, Kate walked briskly to her shop. After entering, she leaned back against the door. She brought the envelope close to her face and inspected her name, which was written in dark, scrawling letters. Turning it over, she walked to her desk, took out her letter opener, and ripped the envelope. Putting the letter opener into her apron pocket, she opened and unfolded the single sheet of paper inside.

Her heart was pounding with fear and anticipation, and she dropped the unread letter onto the table. Closing her eyes, she fell into her chair, letting her head fall back as she looked at the ceiling. *I can't keep living like this, with so much distrust.* Kate looked at the letter as it lay in front of her. She sat up and let her fingers trace the large letters of her name at the top of her page.

She jumped to her feet and walked toward her large worktable. *I have orders I need to finish.* The letter lay on the far side of her table as she began to work. Hope pulled her to read it, but fear seemed to drag her away.

She tried to sketch, but every time she moved her pencil to the blank page, her mind would slip to the words that Boone had asked her to read, and her gaze would be drawn to the folded paper. It haunted her as she started to push fabric through her sewing machine.

The day drew on. She resisted the urge to find out what Boone thought would be important enough to make two copies of. When the sun began to set, she placed a lit lamp beside her sewing machine and sat down. Once again, Kate's eyes were drawn to the letter. Her hands fiddled with the seam of her sleeve, and her knees bounced. She bit at her bottom lip with her teeth.

Boone had never been so anxious in his life as he waited for Kate to read his letter. He hoped she would understand his feelings and, better yet, return them. It seemed impossible to try not to think about what would happen if she rejected him, and he couldn't keep his mind from rehearsing scenario after scenario.

After giving her the letter, he had made sure Kate reached her shop safely. When she had passed by the boarding house, he saw Dixon and his brother exit the saloon. He was sure she had seen as well, but she had kept walking to her shop, and the men had put him on edge. So, unknown to Kate, he had decided to watch over her for the rest of the day.

The daylight was fading as he glanced toward the dress shop again—still as uneventful as it had been all afternoon. But Boone didn't mind at all. As long as Kate was safe, he was content.

"There you are, Boone," Charlotte said, coming to stand beside him with a quizzical look on her face. "How long have you been leanin' against this building?"

"About 20 minutes. I was leaning against the feed store for an hour though," Boone said, pointing.

Charlotte sighed. "While I admire your dedication to keep Kate safe, Jesse and I need your assistance. He finished building the table for his and Beth's home, but he can't load it into the wagon alone."

"Can you ask one of your other patrons?" Boone asked, uninterested in leaving his self-assigned post.

"I already did."

"Can it wait till later?"

"Boone Carson, I'm sure Kate will be fine for a few minutes."

He sighed in frustration. "Fine. I'll give you ten minutes, then I'm coming back here."

Kate couldn't take it any longer.

"Fine! I'll read the blasted letter, but only because I gave him my word," she said to the shop. After grabbing it, she sat down at her sewing desk again and unfolded the letter.

Her heart thundered in her chest, but she took a deep breath and started reading:

My dearest Kate,
I wrote a copy of this letter and sent it to my
mama. This copy is for you.

Dear Mama and Pa,
The things I am going to say in this letter
might convince you that I have gone mad,
and in a way, that is exactly what has hap-
pened. This is my second attempt at writing
this letter. The first letter met its untimely
fate by being ripped to shreds and plunged

into a cup of water. The woman responsible for this is Kate Morrison, and I have fallen completely in love with her.

I know this may come as a shock, given my previous letters. And I know I asked you to arrange a marriage for me because I believed I couldn't offer any woman the decency of a proper courtship. I truly thought I would never find happiness for the rest of my life.

I was wrong. Not only did I find happiness but I also found love that could sustain me for the rest of my life. Whenever I'm with Kate, I am filled with joy! I plead with you both to do whatever is necessary to end the arranged marriage. I no longer want it, and I'm a fool to have ever asked it of you.

Kate is compassionate, stubborn, beautiful, and full of life. The first time I met her, I was gravely injured, and she was the one who saved my life. She had to threaten me with a needle to get me to cooperate, but I've realized that I love her ability to solve any problem she's faced with—even if her methods are strange. She works for her own living and makes sure no one is going to stop her from achieving her dreams. I admire her drive and love of hard work. She is caring and selfless and willing to help anyone, but she won't allow people to push her around.

After the war, I was a shell of the man I used to be, but Kate has helped me change how I see the world. She's opened my eyes to the beautiful things around me and has given me a reason to live again.

I am in the fight of my life right now, and I am terrified that I will lose Kate because I asked for this arrangement. I hope to share the depth of my affection with her before you receive this. Should she accept me, I will stay here with her if that's what she wishes.

If she does not share my feelings, I will return home to resume my work on the ranch. However, I refuse to follow through with the arranged marriage. Kate has taught me what true happiness is, and I know I'm capable of finding it for myself, which is precisely what I plan to do. I understand that there may be some difficulty convincing the other side to agree to this. I certainly don't want to hurt this other woman's feelings, but I also don't want to consign either of us to a marriage when I know my heart will not be able to be fully hers. I pray that neither of you will be too angry with me about my decision.

*I love the woman I met here in Brexton, and
if she loves me too, I hope to ask her to be
my wife. My deepest wish is to spend the rest
of my life with her.
All my love, Boone*

Kate read through the letter two more times, her heart pounding more and more each time she did. Boone's words of love and adoration moved her to tears. She knew he cared for her, but she had not realized that the depth of his feelings matched hers. She got off the floor and placed the letter on the table next to Beth's dress.

How stupid! She realized now how wrong she'd been about everything. How could she have compared Boone to Henry? They were nothing alike. She wondered how she ever thought that pushing him away would ever fix the pain of her past. Boone had helped her heal the wounds of her heart just as she had helped to heal his leg and his soul.

Kate started walking to the door, eager to talk with Boone and clear everything up. Then guilt stopped her. She had treated Boone so poorly over the last few weeks. She became aggravated at herself for blocking her own happiness. Kate had fought for her independence by resisting her mother, running away, and setting up a dress shop. Why hadn't she fought for Boone? *How could I have let my parents influence my thinking so heavily even though I did everything I could to be nothing like them? And now, how do I talk to him after everything I put him through?* she asked herself.

Humility crashed through Kate's body. *Just start talking. He'll listen.* Boone loved her. He wouldn't spurn her. He'd told her so with his actions.

She was about to take a step forward when a hand crashed through the glass on the front door. She froze until she heard Dixon's voice coming through the broken window. Kate dropped to the floor and hid behind the back table as the door opened.

"Where'd she go?" Dixon's slurred voice called through the darkness.

"I don't see 'er." Another responded, sounding just as drunk.

"Well, she's gotta be here. No one's seen her since this mornin', and her guard dog ain't around." She heard him bump into a table.

"Lucky for ya, hey Lez?" The other man chuckled.

"Shut up and keep lookin'."

The two men bumped around the shop while Kate looked for an escape.

"Why she got so much stuff in here?" the unknown man said as he walked into another dress form.

"I dunno, Mathias. Issa dress shop."

"Don't call me Mathias here!"

After weighing her limited options, Kate decided her best chance was to escape out the back door. It was locked, and the key was on the table she was hiding under. A dress form stood in front of the table, and she hoped it would keep Dixon from seeing her hand. She jumped as a small table crashed to the ground. Reaching up as quietly as she could, she felt around till her fingers touched the key. She only had moments before they stumbled to her corner.

She prayed their impaired state would slow them down and allow her to get away.

Mustering her courage, Kate leaped to her feet and dashed to the door.

"There she is! Catch 'er!" Dixon shouted.

Kate reached the door and inserted the key into the lock, but her fingers were trembling, and the task took too long. Right as she turned the lock, the man named Mathias grabbed her arm, pulling her to him and covering her mouth with his other hand. She writhed around trying to escape, but the man holding her squeezed her arms till she whimpered in pain.

"Let's tie 'er up," Dixon said, ripping some of her fabric into long strips. They tied her hands and feet and gagged her mouth. She twisted and turned and fought as hard as she could, but the men worked together till all she could do was wiggle around.

Dixon leaned close, and Kate's stomach heaved from the stench of his breath.

"I gotcha now, Kate," he said.

Thrashing around again, Kate tried to yell for help, but the gag muffled her screams. She only stopped when Dixon slapped her face with the back of his hand. All she could do was glare as pain clouded her vision.

While she was stunned, the men half carried, half dragged her out the back door of her shop and through a few bushes until they reached a pair of horses. Mathias mounted one, and together, the men awkwardly draped her over his lap.

"Ya better be worth it," Dixon growled into her face as he tied her hands to the saddle strap. Her eyes watered from the foul smell, and her tears lingered as the men took her away into the darkness.

Twenty

Boone repeatedly tapped his foot while the wagon lumbered along down the road to Kate's shop. In the end, the task took much longer than any of them had thought it would. Instead of just loading the cart, Jesse had asked Boone to come with him to unload the table and a few other pieces of furniture. They were further delayed when extra help was needed to take a few heavier items into the house. Over an hour later, they were finally on their way back to the boarding house, and only the tiniest glow of light remained on the horizon while the rest of the sky was an ominous black.

"Can you go any faster?" Boone asked Jesse impatiently.

"We'll be there shortly. I'm sure Miss Morrison is just fine."

Boone wanted to agree with him, but something in his gut wouldn't settle. As they came around the corner, Boone could make out the outline of Kate's shop, but something didn't seem right.

Darkness had fallen, and there was almost no moonlight, but the shop's windows were still dark. Had Kate come home while he'd been helping Jesse? Had she fallen asleep in her shop? His mind tried to come up with a reasonable explanation, but his intuition whispered that something was wrong—very wrong.

Dread filled him, and he leapt from the wagon, ignoring Jesse's cry of protest. Boone sprinted as fast as he could to the shop's door. His heart constricted when he noticed it was slightly ajar, and he burst into the shop while calling Kate's name. He heard no reply other than the sound of something cracking under his boots. Tentatively, he looked down.

Broken glass.

His heart dropped when he looked at the door and realized one of the panes of glass had been shattered. Boone rushed around the shop, terrified of what he might find. Even in the near-complete darkness, he could tell Kate's once beautiful shop was now a disaster.

"Kate? Kate!" Boone knew calling for her was futile, but he needed to be sure. He lit a lantern, and the shadows heightened the chaos as he looked around. He searched everywhere, lifting up dress forms and looking under tables. All the while, he was filled with terror for Kate's safety and rage at Dixon for what he'd surely done. But most of all, Boone raged at himself for leaving. None of this would have happened if he'd been watching.

"Boone!" Jesse said, not bothering to hide his irritation. "What's gotten into you?" But his mouth fell open as he looked around the wrecked shop. "Oh no. Do you think it was—,"

"Dixon. I know it." Boone said, as something on the back table caught his eye.

"But do you know if he took her? Maybe she escaped and went back to the boarding house," Jesse said, putting his hand on Boone's shoulder.

"I don't think so," Boone said, shrugging Jesse's hand off. He held up the open letter Kate had finally taken from him only hours before. Boone took the lantern and walked to the open back door. The key was still in the lock.

They inspected the ground together, finding two fresh sets of large boot prints. They followed the tracks away from the shop and through the bushes to the edge of the town. Here, the tracks met hoof prints.

"Boone, look," Jesse said, pointing to a few branches on the bushes. Boone brought the lantern closer and saw what Jesse was pointing at. Blue fabric with little white flowers. The same print that Kate had been wearing that day. Boone stood straight and fought the urge to shout all his fear and anger into the night. Turning around, he ran back to the shop, Jesse right behind him.

"I need you to get Sheriff Garrett and some other men and bring them to Dixon's property."

Jesse nodded. "What are you gonna do?"

"I'm going straight there. He's the worst sort of degenerate, but he's not stupid. He'll try to leave Brexton as soon as possible to try to avoid being caught." Boone ran into a nearby livery and quickly saddled a horse. "I'm not gonna give him the chance to escape."

"All right. Don't do anything rash, and try to wait for me to round up some men. I'll let Harvey know you borrowed one of his horses," Jesse said.

"Thank you, Jesse. And hurry!" Boone said before urging the horse into a gallop as Jesse ran to the jailhouse.

The wind flew through Boone's hair as horrible images of what Dixon might do flooded his mind. His hands tightened around the reins, his nails digging into his palms. *If he hurts her, I'll kill him.*

Within minutes, Boone arrived at Dixon's property. He saw a light in the barn and dismounted, tying his horse near the house.

Boone snuck up to the barn and peaked into the window. He could see Kate, and he wanted to yell. Although she was standing, her mouth was gagged, and they'd bound her hands and feet, securing her to a post. Glaring at her captors as they stood a few feet away, Boone could see a dark ring appearing around her eye. He wanted to barge in, but he knew his odds were bad until Jesse brought help. Resigned, he sat to wait until he had a better chance.

Kate struggled with the ropes on her hands. They were attached to another short length of rope in front of her so she couldn't move very far from the post. Dixon had switched out the fabric ties for actual ropes as soon as they had arrived at the barn. Kate had attempted to escape during the switch, but her efforts resulted in Dixon beating her a few times. The skin around her eyes was swollen and tender.

Dixon and Mathias worked quickly to pack their horses and load them with supplies. Beside them was a third horse. One she would have to avoid at all costs.

The men were brothers, from what they had said, and while they had been drowning themselves in spirits, they had decided to kidnap her—though she still didn't know why.

"How far do we hafta go?" Mathias asked.

"Prob'ly all night. Someone might try n' chase us for a while."

Mathias scratched his head. "I dunno if she's worth the trouble no more."

"Trust me, she is. She woulda been worth more if my first plan had gone through, but the soldier got in the way of that, so I had'a switch things up."

"What was yer first plan then?"

Dixon glared at Kate and she glared back. "I planned to marry 'er!" he shouted.

"I guess that didn't go well." Mathias let out a snorting laugh. "So yer gonna ransom 'er instead?" he asked, tightening a strap.

"Yep," Dixon said, leaning close to Kate's face. "That's right. I know all about ya, *Miss Morrison.*" He said her name laden with sarcasm, and Kate felt the blood drain from her face. *Just how much does he know?*

"Ya sure we can pull it off, Lez? Kidnappin' and ransomin' is mighty different from robbin' banks."

Kate's mind whirled, trying to put the pieces together. Thankfully, Mathias was just as curious as she was.

"And why her? Why this place?"

Dixon crossed his arms and puffed his chest out. "Simple. Her mama wants her back home."

Kate's eyes went wide with shock.

He knew her mother? She had sent him? Did that mean her mother knew where she was? Her head swam with questions.

"Course, since her fam'ly's wealthy, I always planned to use her to get more. I figured if we married, the payday would never' end. Just a few accidents, and I'd inherit everythin'."

Mathias nodded, but Kate couldn't breathe.

"So, after I tracked 'er down, I used the last of my money and bought a house. But that dirty soldier showed up, and she started chasing him! So I decided to change my plan." He gestured around them.

Kate recovered her composure and sent all the hatred she could at Dixon. The fear now coursing through her body at the thought of being taken away from Boone and sent back to her parents might just terrify her more than the threat Dixon and his brother posed.

"But this'll be my only ransom. It's more work than it's worth. I'd rather go back to robbin' banks again with ya, brother."

"I'll drink to that," Mathias said, producing a bottle of liquor and taking a long swig. "To the Warhol brothers! May we get rich and never be caught."

Kate looked quizzically at Mathias. *Warhol brothers? Robbing banks?*

"Shut up, Mathias," Dixon said, chuckling as he snatched the bottle and took a drink of his own.

Kate struggled against her ropes again, and Dixon came closer to her once more. "I know yer mad now, but no need to worry as long as yer ma and pa pay up." He leered at her, and Kate's stomach heaved.

Dixon started moving closer, his expression changing. His eyes roamed over her. She had seen this look on Dixon's face too many times before, and she began hopping away as far as the short rope and tied feet would let her.

"Keep working, Mathias. I wanna have a little chat with the girl," he said. Licking his lips, he grabbed her, and ran a hand through her hair.

She tried to pull her head away, but Dixon managed to stop her by gripping her hair till she winced. He chuckled as she glared at him. "Really, Kate. If ya jus' hold still, I'll take this off," he said, stroking the strap of the gag that was tight against her cheek.

Dixon moved closer and pinned her legs beneath his own. One of his hands grabbed her jaw and turned her to face him. The other hand resumed stroking the rope on her face and in her mouth. "Such a beauty. Shame yer more trouble than yer worth."

Dixon leaned in, and Kate squirmed at his nearness. She knew she had to use every possible second to try and get free before he took the gag off to kiss her—or worse. Kate's mind called out for Boone. She knew he would look for her eventually, but she also knew he probably wouldn't find her in time. Bolstering her remaining courage, she gave Dixon what she hoped was her most withering glare.

He merely sent her a lecherous smile and slipped the gag out of her mouth, moving his head closer to hers. But as soon as the gag was gone, Kate spat in his face. Dixon let go of her and reeled back a few steps. Fury raging in his eyes.

Kate exploded. "You are an even bigger idiot than I thought if you think I was going to come quietly. I would rather die!" she shouted at him.

Dixon immediately jumped forward and clamped his hand down on her mouth to try and silence her, but she bit the palm of his hand as hard as she could. He shouted in pain and pulled away. But before she could act again, the back of Dixon's hand smacked her face and she fell to her knees, the short rope pulling her bound hands above her.

In her haze of pain, Kate heard a shout of fury. She turned her head toward the sound just as the barn doors flew open and a man rushed at Dixon.

"Boone!" she said, her heart leaping.

Boone caught Dixon by surprise and delivered a brutal blow to the side of his head. The foul man fell over, dazed, and rolled to his side. Mathias jumped at Boone, catching him around the chest, causing the pair to fall backward onto the floor. They were a mess of fists, legs, and dirt, and Kate felt powerless to help. After about a minute, she heard the crushing sound of a bone breaking. Mathias's string of profanities and painful howls gave her relief as Boone got to his feet. He began to advance toward Dixon, who was holding his head and steadying himself on a stall.

"Stay down, Dixon. Or should I say Warhol? I beat you before, and I can do it again," Boone said, his arms up, ready for an attack.

Boone's words seemed to rally Dixon's senses. "I'll kill ya!" Dixon barreled forward with a roar.

"Boone!" Kate screamed.

But Boone was ready for the assault. He caught Dixon in the chin with a powerful upward blow, sending him backward. Boone wasted no time and advanced. His fist met with Dixon's face and then his stomach. He doubled over, and Boone brought his fist down on the back of Dixon's neck.

But they had moved too close to Mathias, who swiped Boone's feet out from under him. Dixon took advantage of Boone's fall and ran to his horse, looking for something in the saddle bags.

Kate's dizziness had finally faded, and she pulled herself up by the rope she was tied to. Although it had hurt, her fall to the ground had loosened the binding. While wriggling her hands to get free, she looked around for a weapon. Everything useful was out of her reach, and she groaned in frustration. Boone leapt to his feet and, seeing that Dixon was occupied, turned toward Kate. But the distinct and familiar click of a revolver's hammer being pulled back stopped Boone in his tracks.

"I figured we'd run into trouble with ya, soldier. Jus' not this soon." Dixon stumbled to the side and waved the gun precariously.

Kate hid behind the post still tried to loosen her bindings and watched Boone put his hands in the air and take a few steps away from her.

"Be careful with that, Dixon," Boone said. "You don't want to add murder to your list of crimes."

"Won't be murder. If I do get caught, you'll be dead, and who's gonna argue when I say it was self-defense?" He laughed, continuing to wave the weapon around.

Kate ducked low, and Dixon pointed it in her direction.

"You leave Kate out of this," Boone shouted, taking more steps away from her.

"I wouldn't shoot her. I still need my payday. But I *will* shoot you." Dixon's voice was menacing, and he leveled the gun in Boone's direction.

Kate couldn't sit and watch Dixon kill Boone, so she did the only thing she could in her trapped state—she pushed at the two metal wheels leaning against the same post she was bound too. She ducked as they fell over, the first landed with a great thump, and the other clanged a split-second later as it landed on the first one.

The distraction made Dixon turn abruptly toward Kate, and he began firing his gun wildly. One bullet struck the barn wall above the window, and another pinged off a tin can at the far end of the barn. Boone shouted and took the opportunity to charge after Dixon. Boone knocked him into the wall, and they fell to the ground. Dixon's gun flew out of his hand as they wrestled in the straw and dirt.

The gun had landed only a few feet in front of Kate, and she realized that with the wheels out of the way, she might be able to reach it. Moving quickly, she pulled at the rope bindings, hoping they would loosen more.

Looking back to Boone and Dixon's fight, she could tell that Boone had the upper hand. He had Dixon against a wall and was landing blow after blow. Dixon's arms were up to shield his face, but Boone was wearing him down. Mathias was still writhing on the ground, but Kate didn't know how long he'd stay there.

Kate needed to get free. Grunting in frustration, she gave a final yank on the rope. She whimpered in pain from the rope burns, but the binds loosened in her hands. She immediately untied her feet and ignored the aching sting on her wrists.

Standing, she looked over and found Boone and Dixon close to her. She held the gun up, catching Boone's eye. But in that moment, Dixon kicked Boone where his wound had been. It had healed, but Kate knew it would still be extremely sore. Boone grunted in pain and dropped to his knees while Dixon dealt a blow to Boone's face, sending him to the ground.

Dixon turned toward Kate and saw she was holding the gun. He advanced toward her.

"Boone get up!" she pleaded. "Boone, please!"

Her cries seemed to get through to him, and he lifted his head. He staggered to his feet and started limping in her direction, but Dixon was just on the other side of the post, his arm reaching for the revolver.

Instinctively, Kate threw the gun toward Boone and tried to move out of Dixon's reach, but she wasn't fast enough.

Dixon pulled a knife from his boot and grabbed her around the waist. Holding her against his chest, he put the knife to her throat. Boone now had the gun in his hand, cocked and pointed at the ground. His expression was intense, but Kate saw the fear in his eyes—fear for her.

"Don't make a move, soldier. Wouldn't want my hand slippin', now, would we?"

Kate sucked in a shaky breath as Dixon pressed the point of the knife against her skin. She looked to Boone, her eyes wide. Dixon walked backward, moving them both to the barn doors.

Boone moved slowly but didn't let go of the gun. "I don't think you wanna do that Dixon. Didn't you say she's gonna bring you a lot of money?"

Kate heard Dixon growl next to her ear, and the pressure of the blade increased for a moment then lessened slightly.

"True enough, soldier. But if you try'n shoot me, you might hit her, or my hand might jerk." The blade jumped at her throat.

Boone's face hardened, and he lowered the gun a little.

Dixon chuckled. "I betcha brought a horse with ya."

Boone inhaled sharply.

"Thought so," Dixon sneered. "Mighty thoughtful of ya, seeing how yer blocking the way to my horse."

They were nearly through the door, and Kate was growing increasingly worried. "Boone," she whispered.

His eyes flared when she said his name, but in a split second, his expression changed. *Did something behind them catch Boone's attention?* He no longer looked agitated. He seemed determined. A smile even threatened to peak though his fierce demeanor. He stopped and dropped the gun to the ground.

Dixon didn't seem to notice the change in Boone's expression and laughed maniacally at his apparent surrender. Fear flowed through Kate. *What was Boone doing?* This was not the scenario she had imagined when she had first seen Boone. She wanted to survive this so she could talk to him about his letter and the wonderful words he had written.

Kate's eyes went wide as she remembered when she'd read the letter. Slowly, she reached into her apron pocket, hoping she was right. Her fingers brushed against something slender and metallic, and her heart beat faster—her letter opener.

She closed her hand around the handle but didn't remove it from her pocket. A few more steps, and they would be outside the barn. She needed to have somewhere to flee if her plan worked.

Dixon nuzzled against her neck. "Nights get cold in the desert, soldier. Good thing the lady and I will be able to keep each other warm." His laughter filled the night as they stepped outside.

"No!" Kate shouted. In one even motion, she brought the letter opener out of her pocket and swung the small weapon down as hard as she could into Dixon's thigh. As Dixon shouted in pain and dropped his arms, Kate stepped to the side and ran. However, her escape was immediately halted when she ran directly into a man's chest.

Looking up and recognizing who it was, she gasped. "Jesse?"

He nodded and led her away from Dixon.

"Stop right there, Lez Dixon," Sheriff Garrett said as he rounded the side of the barn followed by a dozen clicks of various weapons being cocked.

Dixon fell to the ground. Kate's letter opener was still protruding from his leg, and a look of shock was on his face. "She stabbed me," he said, blustering.

"You'll live," the sheriff said, grabbing hold of Dixon and pulling his hands behind his back.

"Kate!" Boone limped out of the barn.

"Boone!" She made her way toward him.

His head turned to the sound of her voice and came over, gathering Kate into his arms. She clung to his neck as the tears began to run down her face, relief washing over her.

"Are you hurt anywhere?" Boone asked, pulling away from her as he brushed the hair from her face. He ignored the activity happening around them. She nodded and showed him her wrists. He gently held them and inspected the angry rope marks there.

"Kate, I'm so sorry I wasn't there. I could have stopped this," he said, tenderly touching the bruises on her face.

The anguish in his voice combined with the realization of what had just transpired overwhelmed Kate. Her breathing became more ragged as she felt her mind slipping and her legs giving out.

"Kate, you're safe. Breathe. Just breathe," Boone said, lowering them both to the ground. His voice pulled her back from the edge of darkness, and his hand cupped her chin and lifted her face to meet his gaze. "You're safe now."

His reassuring voice calmed her heart and when she was ready, he helped her to stand once more.

"I have you," he whispered into her hair.

Sheriff Garrett came over. "How is she, Carson?" he asked.

"I'm a little sore but I think I'll be fine, Sheriff," Kate said. "I'm just a little overwhelmed right now."

The sheriff nodded and looked to Kate. "Would you be up to tellin' me about everything later?"

"I think I can help you with that now, sir," Boone said. "Dixon was hired by Miss Kate's mother to bring her back home. He wanted to marry her for her inheritance but changed his mind to ransoming her when marrying her wasn't going to happen."

The sheriff's eyes widened.

Boone continued. "I think you'll be interested to know that they admitted to robbing banks before you got here. They called themselves the Warhol Brothers."

Kate nodded. "I heard that too."

Sheriff Garrett looked from Boone to Kate in surprise. "Well, I'll be. The Warhol brothers? I got their wanted poster a few months ago. I'll hafta look into that. Thank ya, son. Miss, get some rest now, ya hear?"

"Yes sir," Kate said softly.

Boone pulled her into an embrace as the Sheriff followed his men. They were hauling Dixon and his brother away, both protesting loudly, but Kate no longer listened to any of it. All she cared about was the man who was holding her.

She pulled away slightly to look at him. "Boone...we...we need to talk."

"We will, but not here," he said, giving her a smile that gave her goosebumps. "But first, let's get you home. You're shaking, and Charlotte is probably worried sick."

She knew he was right but didn't want to leave his embrace just then. Mustering every ounce of courage she could, she grabbed his face with her trembling hands and pulled his lips to hers, giving him the sweetest of kisses—pouring her unspoken love and intention into it. She could feel Boone's surprise in his response but he seemed to overcome it quickly and he tightened his hold on her waist, pulling her close.

Kate pulled away, brushing her fingers over his lips. She gazed at him with a slight smile. His eyes blazed with a hopeful warmth that nearly turned her knees to liquid, simultaneously encouraging and terrifying her.

Boone put his arm around her shoulders and began leading her back to his horse. He helped her mount before climbing into the saddle behind her and wrapping his arms around her. While Boone held her, she leaned her back against his chest, holding one of his hands. They rode slowly, neither of them saying a word. Kate's stomach was twisting in anticipation, the strong and steady beat of Boone's heart against her back soothing her own.

After they arrived at the boarding house, Boone indicated to Kate to precede him. She shuffled through the back door into the kitchen, intent to stride straight to the parlor to sit and have a discussion with him, but Beth and Charlotte wrapped her in hugs and tears as soon as she stepped through the door.

Both women's relief was nearly tangible as they expressed their worries and their gratitude for Kate's safety. Kate stole a glance at Boone, who was lingering near the door. She grinned at his expression of annoyance. But when their eyes met, his mouth widened into that same charming smile he saved just for her. She knew he wanted to spend some time alone with her as well. She drew herself out of Charlotte's and Beth's strong grasps and beamed at her dear friends.

"Oh, Kate! We were worried sick," Beth said.

"Oh my, yes!" Charlotte said. "After Jesse came by to recruit some of the patrons for help, I fetched Beth to help soothe my worried heart. But that...well, it didn't work. We've been sitting here crying for an hour. Did that awful man hurt you? Whatever happened?"

Kate glanced over to Boone again, aching to be with him. She hoped he would step in and pull her away to the parlor. As much as she loved her friends, she was impatient to talk about the letter. To know, once and for all, what would happen between her and Boone. She hoped he could see the pleading in her eyes.

He walked over to her and took her hand, pulling her to the side. "I just need a minute Miss Charlotte, Miss Beth."

"Where should we talk?" Kate whispered.

To her surprise, he shook his head. "They need you first. We can talk later when no one can interrupt us."

Kate's eyes narrowed, and her mouth tightened into a pout. "But—"

He kissed her forehead then gave her an encouraging smile. "I have to give more details to the sheriff anyway. I'll be back soon." Boone cupped her cheek and walked out the door.

Kate knew he was right. She turned back to the wide-eyed Charlotte and Beth and took their hands. Together, the women moved to the sit in parlor so Kate could tell them the horrid story.

Twenty-One

Relating the tale to Charlotte and Beth had taken much longer than Kate had thought it would. Beth and Charlotte had both fired constant questions. During that time, Boone had left to talk to the sheriff and then had returned with Jesse.

As soon as the story was finished, Boone walked to Kate and took her hand, pulling her to her feet. He looked to the small group then.

"Thank you all for your help and concern. But now, if you don't mind, Kate and I need a little privacy to have a discussion we've put off for far too long." Kate's heart leaped at his words, her hand clasped in his strong one.

But before anyone moved, Charlotte leaped to her feet. "No!"

Boone turned his head, frowning at Charlotte and looking exasperated. Even Kate felt miffed at her words.

Charlotte sighed and regained her composure. "No," she repeated softer. "It's late, and Kate's had a difficult evening. I'm aware that you two must have many things to discuss, but you both need sleep. We all do, and it's well after time to be in bed."

Boone sent a pointed look toward Charlotte. But she ignored him and continued, her hands now on her hips.

"Being older and therefore wiser, I have a good idea where this talk of yours will end, and I can't in good conscience let you have a conversation that intimate this late at night. Sleep first, then talk." Charlotte looked to Kate then.

Once she got their reluctant nods, Charlotte continued. "Chances are you'll have a more level head then, anyway."

Jesse snickered and Beth stifled a giggle, but they stopped short as Charlotte pointed her finger at them. "That goes for everyone."

"Yes, Mama," Jesse said, grinning widely.

"Now, Jesse, walk Beth home and come back promptly." They both nodded and left, arm in arm. Charlotte then turned back to Kate and Boone.

"Boone Carson," she said, her gaze direct and her voice stern.

Boone's eyebrows raised at the use of his entire name. "Yes, ma'am?" he asked, sounding like a schoolboy about to get in trouble. Kate struggled to keep a straight face.

"Please say goodnight to Miss Morrison," Charlotte said, folding her arms over her chest.

Kate felt terribly self-conscious with Charlotte there, watching them. She fidgeted with her skirt and looked everywhere except at Boone. She heard him chuckle, and she finally looked up. He was smiling down at her, surely understanding her frustrations and shyness.

He held one of her hands loosely in his. "Miss Charlotte, you're denying me the goodnight I planned to give

Miss Kit," he said, his eyes never straying from Kate's face. She blushed under his stare. "I was really looking forward to it," he said, just so Kate could hear. Her heart pounded.

Charlotte's only answer was an impatient sigh, her foot tapping the floor.

Kate didn't know where all her newfound courage came from. It could have been because of the lateness of the hour or perhaps because of what she'd read in Boone's letter. Maybe it was a plethora of things, but without overthinking the cause, she promptly said, "To be honest, Miss Charlotte, I was looking forward to this goodnight as well."

Boone's eyes widened in pleased surprise, and Kate was glad she'd admitted what she'd been thinking.

Charlotte crossed her arms and made a loud tsking sound, but the corner of her mouth twitched a few times as she turned her back on the two of them. "Hurry now, you two."

"Fine, fine," Boone said. He narrowed his eyes, a familiar mischief reflecting in their ocean-colored depths. Kate was thrilled at his expression. The desire swimming in his eyes matched her own.

His thumb stroked the back of her hand he was still holding—his voice low and provocative—hinting at something wonderful to come.

"Goodnight, Kit."

Boone cupped Kate's cheek, and she could feel the warmth of his hand, her heart beginning to race. His thumb caressed the edge of her lower lip. She lifted her chin, and her eyes fluttered shut. The light brush of his lips against the corner of her mouth sent a rush of excitement through her. He moved to the other side before he teased her lower lip. Her breath caught as he pressed his lips to hers, her hands tracing the corded veins in his arms. Goosebumps ran down her spine, and she smiled, returning the kiss.

Hearing Charlotte start blustering, Boone stepped back, a cocky smile donning his face while a furious blush blazed on Kate's as Charlotte stomped toward them.

"I swear you two are going to give me fits," Charlotte said, wagging a finger at Kate and lightly smacking Boone upside the head. Kate, still thinking about the kiss, held her fingers to her lips and walked backward toward the stairs.

"Have a good sleep, Miss Kit. I hope to say goodnight like that to you tomorrow," Boone said, winking at her. Charlotte smacked his arm, and he chuckled as he turned and went into his own room.

Charlotte stared after Boone until he closed his door. Turning and walking to Kate, Charlotte's eyes widened, and she started. "So, there seems to be something I've missed!" She hustled Kate up the stairs to her bedroom.

"You're going to bed right now, but tomorrow you and I are going to have a chat. I'm not blind, Kate. Anyone could see that you and Boone had been getting close, but with all the avoidance and arguing, I wonder what changed."

Kate smiled. *Everything.*

"Now get some rest." She held Kate's face then, her eyes brimming with tears. "I'm only being so strict 'cause I've grown rather fond of you, Kate, and I just want the best for you." She paused and looked down momentarily. "I hope you don't mind that I've begun to think of you as another daughter."

The love in Charlotte's voice brought tears of her own. "Oh, Charlotte! You have been more of a mother to me than my own ever was." She threw her arms around her neck and both women cried softly.

After a while, Charlotte pulled away, wiping her eyes. "Well, now that I'm all sloppy, I'm going to bed, and you oughta do the same." Charlotte left, and Kate nodded, a contented smile on her lips.

Twenty-Two

Kate tried everything she could think of to force her mind to calm itself and let her sleep, but it was a futile battle. She'd been in bed for hours thinking about the things she would say to Boone in the morning.

She wanted to apologize for being so hard-headed and for not listening, and she wanted him to know that she loved him. She sat up, struck with the significance of her feelings. *I love Boone.* The thought filled her mind, and nothing was going to stop her from fighting for what she now understood that she wanted.

She'd stayed up all night, having given up trying to sleep. The sky already showed the first hints of light on the horizon. Sighing, she threw off the covers, put a robe on over her nightgown, and quietly exited her room.

Moving silently, Kate went to the parlor and built up the fire that had died to only a few glowing embers. She stood in front of the fireplace and stared at the flames, letting her mind wander. Unsurprisingly, she found that her thoughts lingered on Boone. All she could think about was him. She wondered whether he had found rest this night, unlike her.

As if her thoughts conjured him, Boone walked into the parlor. They looked at each other for a few moments. She noticed his hair was tousled and boyish; it made him look so adorable, and she just wanted him to hold her. But they needed to talk before anything else could distract her—and Boone was distracting!

So, Kate sat in an armchair next to the fireplace and motioned for him to sit across from her. He sauntered over and started to push the chair closer.

"No!" she said.

Boone's eyes went wide. "Why?"

"Because there are some things I need to say to you, and I think it would be easier for me if you stayed over there."

He chuckled and complied, leaning back and looking at her expectantly.

"I have always been impulsive," Kate told him, but Boone only grinned. "I was when I ran away, and this time was no different. But you have to understand, even though I knew my parent's views on contracts were extreme, I didn't realize how much I had adopted their views. Nor how much of that view I have been pushing onto you, even if I wasn't trying to." She looked away. "And that is not right."

When she looked back, Boone gave her an encouraging smile. Kate took a deep breath.

"Boone, I wanted you to be mine," she said, speaking softly. "One day, I noticed our friendship had changed—had turned into something more—and...I discovered I cared for you. More than I realized. I told myself that wouldn't happen again. Not after Henry."

Boone sat up straight, and the corners of his mouth twitched. She knew she had his full and undivided attention.

"So, when I learned about your arranged marriage, I..." She paused, wondering how frank she should be. But Charlotte's words came back to her, and she felt a surge of courage that gave her the confidence to say what was in her heart. "Well, to be honest, I thought, 'That's it. He belongs to someone else and—'" She paused again. She locked eyes with Boone and whispered, "—I couldn't handle being hurt like that again, so I tried to push you away, to push my feelings for you away.'"

Boone reached out to hold her hand, his gaze intense on her face.

"What about now?" he asked, his voice quiet.

Tell him! her mind screamed. Instead, she said, "I'm not finished."

Boone blew out the breath he had apparently been holding but stayed quiet.

"I thought I had to push you away to make it easier for me, but I was wrong. I assumed you would be just like Henry, and so I treated you as such. Then I tried holding you to the marriage even though it would have made you unhappy. I think I wanted to make you want to leave so it would be easier for me to say goodbye when the time came. But you fought me at every step.

"Unfortunately, I'm more like my parents than I thought, and I refused to listen to you. I tried to control your arrangement...just like my mother tried to control me. I shouldn't have done any of that, and I offer you my sincerest apologies, Boone." Kate rushed on so he wouldn't interrupt again.

"But after I read your letter, I was not sure what to do. My parents' opinions were still in the back of my mind, and I was so confused. But then I remembered something Charlotte had said. She told me to be honest with myself and to think about what *I* wanted in life. To fight for it, no matter what."

When Kate looked into Boone's face, she shivered at the plain adoration in his eyes.

"So here I am, even though I'm impulsive, defensive, highly opinionated, untrusting, and controlling. But I am also persistent, and I'm ready to fight for what I want. So, I'm going to fight for you now because I want you...because I love you."

Boone sat silently, not sure if he had heard her correctly. He had been imagining those words for so long that he couldn't tell whether this was another daydream. As he searched Kate's face, he could see her fierce determination, and he couldn't stop staring. Uncertainty slowly crept into her eyes the longer he was silent, and Boone felt the need to touch her. To reassure both of them that this was real.

He left his chair and knelt at hers, only the armrest separating them. Boone brought his hand up to smooth her hair away from her face before bringing it to her cheek. While he cradled her face in his hands, he searched her eyes. "You love me? Truly?" he asked.

Kate nodded, tears filling her eyes.

"You read the letter?"

"Yes," she whispered.

He pulled her face close to his, only inches apart. "Then you remember the part where I said that I love you?"

She nodded and Boone continued. "Kit, I'm well aware that you are all those things you said, but you are also selfless, determined, caring, and strong, and I love it all. You're the woman I want in my life. Besides, I'm hard-headed, pushy, overprotective, and I probably tease you too much. You'll have to be patient with me. But, like you, I'm also persistent. So I know that no contract will impede me loving you. Trust me on that. I will find a way out of this because I want to marry you. I want to build a life, a home, a family with you. And I really hope you agree to that."

Tears spilled over Kate's cheeks and without a word, she threw her arms around his neck, her lips finding his. Boone's arms wound around her waist, and he pulled her as close as he could despite the armrest.

After a few moments, Boone broke away. His hands caressed her face, and he asked, "I take it that's a yes?" He gave her a mischievous smile. "But if this is how you say no to me, you should definitely say no more often."

She kissed him briefly and smiled against his lips. "Yes, Boone. I would very much like to marry you."

Boone's mouth was on hers again, softer and slower than before.

When they separated, Boone held Kate's hand as he walked her to the bottom of the stairs. He lifted her hand to his lips and kissed it tenderly. When he lowered it, her eyes had darkened, and she seemed worried.

"What is it?" Boone asked.

"My parents would hate this, but I don't really care. However, I am worried about your parents. What will they think of you? Of us? Will they accept us? Or will they disown you?"

Boone chuckled. "If they disapprove, then Charlotte can adopt us both." Kate rolled her eyes, but Boone also saw her body relax. He gripped her hand harder. "Don't worry. I'm sure they'll come to accept it. When they do, I know they are going to love you. Just like I do." He kissed the back of her hand again and smiled.

Kate smiled, nodded, and walked up the stairs. As he watched her go, he hoped his words were true. Everything would work out. It had to.

Twenty-Three

A week had passed, and Kate stood at the other end of the kitchen worktable, rolling out some dough Charlotte had just finished making. Finished pies lined one side of the kitchen, ready to be eaten. Today was Beth and Jesse's wedding, and people bustled about the kitchen. The energy was palpable and filled with joy.

Kate jumped at sudden pounding on the front door.

"Oh, Kate, would you be a dear and answer that? It might be more relatives. Let them know I can't help at the moment." Charlotte said. She was hands deep in dough.

Kate nodded and dusted the flour off her hands, pushed the hair out of her face, and tried to smooth out the front of her dress.

She rushed through the kitchen door into the parlor but halted as she collided with Boone. After his and Kate's new arrangement, Charlotte had made him find another place to stay, so Kate was happy anytime she could see him.

"Well, what a pleasant surprise." Boone chuckled as he bent toward her. He kissed her twice in quick succession and was about to give a third when the pounding grew in demand.

"I'm sorry. I have to answer that." Kate kissed his cheek before brushing past him toward the door.

"You've got something on your face." He said with a chuckle as he made his way through the same door she left. There was another pounding, and Kate rushed past the parlor.

"Hello. Are you here for the wedding?" Kate asked as she pulled the door open with a smile. A man and woman stood in the doorway. The man was tall and well dressed, with salt-and-pepper hair and an unreadable face, which somewhat unnerved Kate. The woman, however, was short and had a warm but worried expression. Her big blue eyes almost reminded Kate of Boone's. The dress she wore was crisp and well made, but she seemed to be worried based on how her hands fiddled with the hem of her shirtwaist.

"No," the woman said. "We are looking for our son. He told us he was in Brexton, staying at a boarding house run by a woman named Charlotte Conrad," the woman said as her eyes darted toward the sign next to the door.

"I'm sorry. We're a little busy around here right now. Why don't you come in, and we will see what we can find out." Kate stepped back and opened the door wide to let them in.

"Thank you," the woman said and walked in, closely followed by her husband. They sat down, and the woman turned to Kate. "If you don't mind my asking, who's getting married today?" The woman seemed almost desperate.

"It's no problem. Charlotte's son, Jesse is marrying Beth Wallace later this afternoon," Kate said. To her surprise, the woman looked to her husband and sighed in both relief and trepidation. "How nice," she said softly.

"Yes." Confusion filled Kate. "May I ask who your son is? I have been here for a time, and I might know him."

"Oh yes, how silly of me," the woman said, offering a small smile. "I am Winnie Carson, and this is my husband Miles." She gestured to the man next to her, who nodded. "We are looking for our son Boone. Do you know him?"

Kate felt her heart jump into her throat. Her chest tightened, and her voice was of no use. She nodded slowly.

"Oh, good. Do you know where he is?" Winnie Carson's eyes darted around the room, as if looking for him.

Kate swallowed hard. "I saw him only moments ago. He shouldn't be too hard to find. If you don't mind waiting here, I can go look for him," she said, turning to go to the kitchen.

"That would be wonderful, thank you," Mrs. Carson gushed, a relieved smile on her face.

Kate walked numbly through the dining room and into the kitchen. Her stomach twisted into knots, and her mind raced. Boone's mother must not have liked what she read in his last letter. Would they reject Kate and not allow Boone to marry her? Her heart pounded in her chest, and her eyes burned.

"Who was at the door?" Charlotte asked as Kate entered.

"Boone's parents. They're looking for him." Kate felt dazed.

If Charlotte was surprised, she didn't show it, although Kate saw the slightest of smiles crease the corner of her mouth.

"He just went out back to help Jesse get things set up for the wedding."

"Thank you," Kate said, heading toward the back door in the kitchen.

Kate glimpsed her reflection in the window near the back door before she left. She looked an absolute mess. Flour was all over her face, bits of hair were sticking out of the bun she had fastened, and she knew her dress was covered in crumbs. *This was not the first impression I wanted to give his parents.* She shook her head and opened the door. Right away, she saw Boone step into the barn.

"Boone, wait," she rushed forward, hoping to catch him. He popped his head back through the door and smiled when he saw her chasing him.

"Come to finish that conversation we were having before you had to answer the door?" He smiled, and she felt her body begin to warm, even despite her nerves.

"It...it's actually about who was at the door."

His brow furrowed. "Who was it?" He took hold of her arms and pulled her close, his eyes searching hers.

"Your parents." She pushed herself out of his grip "They are in the parlor waiting for you."

His eyes grew wide. "Come with me." He reached for her hand, but she pulled it away.

"I should go see if Charlotte needs any more help in the kitchen, and Beth and I are going to pick wildflowers. I'll see you later." She couldn't meet his eyes. She felt like a complete mess, and now his parents were here. Dread pooled in the pit of her stomach as she rushed away from him.

That woman is going to drive me insane. Boone watched Kate. Her head was down, and her arms were wrapped around herself, as if she was protecting herself from some unseen pain. That only made him want to run after her more.

He knew he didn't want to meet Kate's family, knowing how they'd treated her all her life. Perhaps she was afraid to meet his parents, since she was the reason that he had broken his arrangement. He knew his parents were probably confused, even irritated, but Boone wasn't worried. They would accept his decision and come to love Kate as a daughter because they were good people and loving parents. Boone shook his head as he climbed the stairs to enter the back of the boarding house. *But what am I going to say to my Mama?*

He made his way to the parlor. Plain as day, there stood his parents, his mama pouring over what he could only assume was his last letter and his pa standing just behind her, his hand rested on her shoulder. Despite his worry, Boone smiled while watching them. One day he hoped to be as happy as his parents were. He wished Kate had stayed with him so he could introduce her.

Boone closed the door behind him and cleared his throat.

"Mama, Pa, what are you doing here?" he asked, though he could guess at the answer to his own question.

His mama looked up at him. Her deep blue eyes, like his own, flashed.

"Boone Carson, why don't you tell us? First you ask for us to arrange a marriage for you. And that is what we did, but months went by and nothing—no word from you. Then you sent the one about wanting to stay for your friend's wedding. It was hard. I wanted you home, but I tried to understand that you were trying to be there for your friend." His mama was clearly frustrated, and he decided that perhaps it was safer for Kate to have gone to pick flowers for Beth instead of coming into the house with him. "You said in one letter that you wanted us to help you, then you weren't sure, and now you're just done with it? Are you sure you aren't having jitters? And what about the last letter you sent me?" Winnie waved it in his face. He knew what it said. Boone had debated over every word.

"Things changed, Mama. I told you that in my letter. I know an agreement was made, but I can't change how I feel about Kate." Boone looked at each of his parents.

"Boone, you don't seem to understand. The family that we arranged the marriage with is insisting that the agreement is binding, and you can't back out."

Boone felt his heart drop, but he ignored it. He had promised Kate he would fix this. "Then we will have to work something else out because I have found the woman I want to marry." His fists balled at his sides as he tried to control the anger that rose within him.

"They are saying they will wait as long as you need to change your mind." She paused. "They think you will come around and realize you committed to that marriage when we met with them several months ago. According to them, a handshake is as binding as a signature."

Boone studied his mama. Something turned inside of Boone. Kate had mentioned that her parents had similar views. Boone shook his head. *Too many people are too strict with marriage contracts.*

"I'm sorry, but I don't care what they think. I have found the woman I love, and I intend to marry her. Nothing they say will change my mind."

Kate entered through the kitchen and found Charlotte pressed up against the door that led to the rest of the house. She laid the wildflowers she had picked for Beth's bouquet on the table.

"Charlotte, what are you doing?" Kate tried to hold back the laugh that filtered through her voice.

Charlotte straightened, brushing her hair out of her face and looking like a child who had been caught with a hand in the cookie jar.

"It's Boone. His parents want him to honor the marriage arrangement, but he is refusing because he wants to marry you." Charlotte smiled.

Kate's cheeks burned, and her heart pounded in her chest.

"They are telling him about the young woman they found for him, but he won't have any of it." Charlotte waved Kate forward.

Kate knew how inappropriate it was to eavesdrop, but she couldn't help the anxious curiosity that pulled her toward the door.

Mrs. Carson's voice was pleading. "You don't even want to see a picture of the young lady? Her mother gave it to me on my last visit with her. She is a beautiful woman; I am sure you will be happy together."

"No, Mama, I don't want to see it. I don't want to know anything about her. It makes no difference, and we won't be happy together. I am going to marry Kate."

"Her mother, Gurty, was pleased with the picture I gave them of you. She was happy her little Kitty would have such a handsome husband."

Kate froze. Her lungs wouldn't take air, and she felt her mouth fall open. A suspicion in her mind began to grow and with it, odd delight. But she had to be sure.

Composing herself, Kate looked at Charlotte. "Did they mention what the young lady's name is?" Kate tried to remember what Boone had told her about his arrangement.

"Yes," Charlotte said slowly, her eyebrows pinched together. "I believe they said her name was Katarina Kingston."

Kate stepped away from the door as she struggled to breathe evenly. *They have a photograph. How did they not know?* She checked her appearance again in the window. Her face was still covered in flour, and her hair was sticking out, even looking gray in some places. *Perhaps it is because I look like I slept in the kitchen.* She went to the water bucket and splashed her face. Pulling the pins from her bun, she unwound the braid till her hair hung in long waves down her back.

"Trying to make yourself more presentable?" Charlotte asked with a grin and a wink.

Kate nodded gently as her fingers deftly worked her hair into a braided bun at the base of her neck. Satisfied, she went to the door and paused for a moment. Her heart pounded furiously. She took a deep breath before she pushed her way into the parlor.

"Kate!" Boone smiled as he watched her enter the room.

"Mama, Pa. This is Kate Morrison, the woman I have been trying to tell you about." He took her hand and kissed it.

Boone's mother sucked in a breath. Her hand flew to her mouth, and her eyes grew wide.

Kate squeezed Boone's hand and prayed for strength.

"Hello Mr. and Mrs. Carson." Kate tried to smile.

Boone's father looked from Boone to Kate, then to his wife. "Winnie, do you mind if I see that picture again?"

Without a word, she passed the black-and-white photo to her husband. He studied it for a time, occasionally glancing up at Kate.

"Son, I would strongly urge you to look at this photograph," Boone's father said, holding it out to Boone. A slight smile glinted in the creases around his eyes.

"Why?" Boone's eyes narrowed as he reached for the offered photo, never letting go of Kate.

She watched his eyes lower toward it. Kate recognized it immediately. Her mother had had the photo commissioned for her sixteenth birthday. Kate sighed. The girl in the photo was more youthful, but it was still Kate.

Boone's eyes, clearly shocked, looked at the photo and then back at Kate.

Kate leaned closer and spoke softly to Boone. "I told you my mother arranged another marriage for me. That's why I left." Then, she straightened her spine and cleared her throat. "Mr. and Mrs. Carson, my full name is Katarina Kingston."

"Wait. Are you telling me that this whole time you were the woman I was engaged to?" Boone looked like he needed to sit down, and Kate couldn't help but smile as she nodded her head.

"So, all the nonsense you put me through? Pointless?" Boone was looking at her like she had two heads, and the Carson's didn't look much different. She grimaced and turned to Boone's parents. She took a deep breath and tried her best to explain that after hearing about her second arrangement, she had run away without knowing any of the details.

"What do you mean you left?" Boone's mother asked.

"Exactly what I said, Mrs. Carson. When I found out my mother had arranged yet another marriage for me, I left. I didn't want to get married. I was engaged once before, and he left me." Kate tried to swallow the emotion in her throat.

"So, all the times I asked to meet you, that's why your mother avoided it. You weren't there?"

"I am sure she made up some frilly excuse, but yes, that is why. I left the same night I found out." Kate looked down at the hand Boone was still holding. "I had given up on marriage and a family because I didn't want to be hurt again. It took a lot for Boone to change my mind." Her gaze trailed up to his face, which was filled with wonder. How she loved this man. "But I am so glad he did." She finished in a whisper, her heart pounding.

Kate swallowed and cleared her throat before turning back to look at his parents.

"I am sorry for all the confusion I have caused, but if he will have me, it would be my honor to uphold the agreement between our families."

Boone pulled her into his arms, and he held her tightly, the warmth and safety she felt within them sending shivers down her spine. The heat of his breath brushed her cheek as he whispered in her ear.

"Is that the only reason you want to marry me?"

She couldn't help the smile that spread across her face as they pulled apart.

"Well, that seems to have worked out," Mrs. Carson said, approaching them. "Perhaps it wasn't the worst thing in the world that you left, my dear. You found your way to your intended and found love without the extra pressure." Mrs. Carson smiled at the two of them for a moment before she turned businesslike. "Now, Boone, when should we expect you home from the wedding? You can't stay here together anymore," his mother said, a knowing smile on her face even as she rushed forward to embrace Kate.

Kate gladly accepted the affection; she had worried that Boone's mother might react like her own mother. But this woman was warm, and Kate hoped to have a wonderful relationship with her.

Kate looked up at Boone. She didn't want to leave Brexton. She'd built the life she had always dreamed of here, and she was happy. *But if he insisted on going back, what should I do?*

"Don't worry. The owner of this boarding house wouldn't have allowed that. I have permission from a family to stay with them while Kate is in the boarding house. And we haven't talked about it yet, but I was thinking we would live here. Kate has a thriving business, and we both have wonderful friends," Boone said, his eyes locked on his parents.

Kate's heart swelled. She could kiss him for what he'd just said.

"How does that sound?" Boone said, finally looking down at her.

"It sounds wonderful," Kate said, her eyes bright with happiness.

"What about your responsibilities on the ranch, son?" His father took a step forward.

"You know Daniel has always wanted to run the ranch," Boone said.

"Boone, one of the reasons her parents picked you was because you were the heir to the ranch. I doubt they will agree if you give that up."

Kate stepped forward. "For once, they aren't going to be the ones to make that choice."

Later that night, Kate sat at one of the long tables watching people dance in the radiance of the setting sun. Beth and Jesse's wedding had been perfect—tears and smiles had been shared by all. Boone had looked downright uncomfortable in his dress suit, but Kate had admired how it enhanced the blue in his eyes. The dinner had been just as wonderful, thanks to the tireless work of Charlotte and the other women.

But Boone had disappeared right after, and Kate hadn't seen him since. She scanned the group of people in attendance. Charlotte was talking with Beth's mother, and Boone's parents were on the dance floor. Mr. Carson's arms were wrapped around his wife like she was the most precious person in the world. Together, they swayed to the music that poured from the band's instruments, and Kate thought about her own parents. She couldn't remember a time her father had ever held her mother like that. In fact, Kate wasn't sure she had ever seen them show any kind of affection for each other. In that moment, Kate's heart hurt for her them. Although they had been married for many years, they had never found the kind of love that she now had with Boone. Remembering her parents' sad example, Kate was baffled that her mother had twice tried to push Kate into a similar loveless marriage.

Kate was startled from her thoughts when she felt warm, powerful hands slip around her waist and a heated breath push through her hair.

"Come away with me, my love."

Kate smiled as she leaned into Boone's arms.

"And where would we go, Mr. Carson?" She turned her head toward him, and he kissed her cheek.

"That is a secret," he said, moving his hands up to tie a piece of cloth around her eyes.

"Boone, what are you doing?" she said, laughing as she tried to pull the cloth away.

"It's a surprise. No peeking!"

Kate sighed but reluctantly did as he asked.

He linked her arm through his and pulled her from her chair. As they walked, the light and sounds of the celebration by the boarding house faded.

"Where are you taking me?"

"Don't worry, it isn't much farther." She could hear the smile in his voice, but there was also a slight quiver. Was he nervous or excited?

"Now stop there and wait until I tell you to take off the blindfold." He sounded almost giddy, but Kate couldn't help the roll of anxiety that rushed through her.

"Boone, what is going on?" she asked.

Kate's heart pounded in her chest as she heard him moving around her.

"You can take it off now." His voice was low.

Kate's breath caught after she pulled the cloth from her eyes. Boone was standing in front of her, grinning. They stood on a blanket surrounded by a circle of candles, wildflowers strewn around their feet. Kate could still hear the faint sounds of the celebration behind her, and she knew they weren't too far from town. She looked to Boone, who was beaming at her. *Did he do this himself?* The thought endeared him to her even more.

"What is this?" Kate looked around and then turned back to Boone, who was now moving toward her.

"I know we already had this conversation with my parents, but I want you to know that this is up to you. If you told me now that you wanted nothing more to do with me, I would leave and never come back, contract or no. But I love you with all that I am." He took her into his arms and took a deep breath before continuing. "Will you make me the happiest man in the world and agree to be my wife?" His eyes were the deepest blue she had ever seen and were full of all the hope and love she could ever imagine.

Tears spilled down her cheeks, and her heart pounded in her chest. But she couldn't get the words past the lump in her throat. She pulled his face to hers and kissed him, pouring all her feelings into the exchange. She wanted him to know how desperately she wanted to have a life with him.

"Yes, I will marry you," she whispered, pulling away from him but not wanting to let go.

Boone sat on the blanket, and Kate sat beside him. She wasn't sure how much time had passed as they kissed and discussed their plans about staying in Brexton. When they got on the subject of their wedding, Boone asked Kate about her family.

"Would you want them to come?"

Kate paused. The only person from her family she might have wanted to share that day with was her brother, Monty.

She smiled. "No. Everyone I care about is already here."

They eventually agreed on just having a simple ceremony here in Brexton: just his parents and a few of their close friends. Their wedding would be nothing as grand as Beth and Jesse's, but it sounded perfect to Kate.

They spoke together quietly after that, Boone never letting her go. For the first time in her life, Kate felt safe and wonderfully content.

"We should go back," Boone said, nudging her head with his shoulders.

"We should," Kate said, but she made no move to leave.

Boone chuckled. "I love you," he said as he pulled her closer and kissed the top of her head.

"I love you, too," she said. Her eyes were closed, but she smiled up at him, loving the way she felt when he was near.

"So, what should I call you now? Katarina?"

Kate sat up and sent a mischievous smile to Boone. "You know, I think I like Kit," she said. They both laughed.

As she snuggled back into his arms, sounds from the celebrations washed over them, and visions of what their own wedding would be like flashed through Kate's mind. She thought back on everything she had gone through since Boone arrived in Brexton. All the misunderstandings and pain—but also all the laughter and joy. When she left home, she thought she was running from her past. But being here with Boone, she could see that she had really been running toward her future.

Kate listened to the rumble of her beloved Boone's voice as he painted pictures of the life they would have together and the joy that awaited them. Their unexpected arrangement had truly helped her find her happiness. And knowing that, all Kate could do was smile.

So, she did.

Acknowledgments

Logan, Mitch, Stephanie, Scott, David, Mackenzie, Meghan, and Haley.

You are the beautiful people who supported and encouraged us the most through this labor of love. We thank you from the bottom of our hearts.

About the Authors

Samantha and Michelle have been close friends for over 20 years. Co-authoring this novella has been a fun and challenging experience for both of them. *An Unexpected Arrangement* is their debut publication.

Samantha A. Curtis

Samantha was born and raised in southern Alberta, Canada, where she continues to live with her husband, three children, and dog. She has always loved reading just about anything she could get her hands on. Samantha loves music, dancing, and game nights. She has been writing since junior high school and is thrilled to finally be able to tell people, "I wrote a book, and here it is!"

Instagram: @samantha.a.curtis.writes
Email: samantha.a.curtis.author@gmail.com

Michelle Huntstrom

Michelle Huntstrom lives in the windy Southern Alberta prairies. With a pristine view of the Rocky Mountains on the horizon, she loves creating stories that make readers' hearts giddy with a splash of romance. When Michelle isn't writing, she's spending time with her husband, two children, and small dog. She's a self-taught pianist, intermediate crafter, and an all-out homebody—though her ideal vacation is lounging somewhere with a pile of good books.

Instagram: @michellehuntstrom_writes
Email: michelle.huntstrom@gmail.com
Goodreads: www.goodreads.com/michelle_huntstrom

www.ingramcontent.com/pod-product-compliance
Lightning Source LLC
Chambersburg PA
CBHW061201210726
48294CB00006B/1707